NIC'S SUITE SANTA

A MONTANA WEEKEND NOVELLA

CYNTHIA BRUNER

Nic's Suite Santa

A MONTANA WEEKEND NOVELLA

Published by Montana Inspired Arts

Cover by Robin Ludwig Design.

Hymn lyrics taken from "It Came Upon The Midnight Clear" by Richard S. Willis and Edmond H. Sears (1850) and "O Holy Night" Placide Clappeau, French (1847), English translation John S. Dwight (1855).

ISBN: 9781790451753

Printed in the U.S.A.

FRIDAY

Her sister's hand hovered over the hotel room lock. "This is a suite," she said.

"Yes, Lauren, you already mentioned that." The two bags Nic Benedict carried were pulling on her arms like impatient toddlers. She was more than ready to get inside and set them down.

"Did I mention there are two babysitters now?"

"Yes, Lauren. And I assume there's a problem with that or you wouldn't be bringing it up. Is it some smelly old aunt who chain smokes? I'll lock her out on the patio. Just let me inside, my arms are killing me."

Lauren shook her head, a tiny little movement she used to ward off embarrassment. "Shh. Someone's going to hear you."

"Then let me inside and I'll be quiet."

Lauren looked at the room's key card. Her shiny brown hair fell like a curtain, shielding her expression from her younger sister. Just about when Nic was going to grab the card and open the door herself, Lauren added with a forced brightness, "There are two rooms in the suite. You get your own room. There are going to be a lot of kids, and they wouldn't all fit if you weren't in a suite."

"Open the door," Nic said. Her stern voice usually didn't work on Lauren. After all, she'd learned it from Lauren in the first place. But she was lucky this time, and her sister finally slid the key card into its slot.

Before Lauren had time to change her mind, Nic lunged forward, opened the door, and pushed inside, ignoring the little groan her sister let out.

It was indeed a suite. What she saw looked about the size of a normal hotel room, but without the beds. Instead, there was a large sofa and a breakfast bar. And sprawled across the sofa, with one worn and dirty-looking hiking boot up on the cushion, was Mark.

Time folded back upon itself. He was at once so familiar, as familiar as her own face in the mirror, and a stranger. She had moved on. But being around him felt like she'd just experienced time travel, and it made her a little queasy.

He waved. Nic turned to her sister, who was looking a little red in the face. "I want my own room," Nic informed her. Her voice, betraying her emotions, was already starting to shake. She wished again that she could deal with her nerves without everyone and their brothers knowing she was struggling.

"You have your own room," Lauren said brightly. "Look over there, you can see there are two separate bedrooms."

"If I bother you, you could always use one of the chairs to barricade me inside my room," Mark offered from behind her.

Lauren rolled her eyes, and Nic didn't need to see the grin on Mark's face to know it was there. She heard it in the tone of his voice. She dropped her bags where she stood and took one step closer to her sister. Even now, wearing boots with a substantial heel, she still had to look up at her. "What were you thinking?" she whispered.

"I'm sorry, Nic. We had two rooms booked, but then Tracie decided to come at the last minute, so she needed one of them. The hotel offered us this suite for the same price. This room should be great when we get all the kids together."

Nic swept a strand of dark-brown hair behind her ear, tucked her coat tightly around her, and crossed her arms over it. "There's got to be another place to stay." Then she mouthed, "Don't do this to me."

Lauren bit her lip. Her perfect lipstick didn't budge. "You could stay with Chris and me."

"There's no place else?"

"No." Lauren looked down. "Most places in Helena are full, too. If I could, I'd get you a room, I really would. I just can't. We can't. I mean—"

"I don't want to stay with you and Chris. You guys are newlyweds, for heaven's sake."

"Hey, Nic, you and I will have chaperones, you know," Mark called out. Nic couldn't believe he was still listening in, even though the conversation was obviously none of his business. "At least half a dozen chaperones. Short ones."

Nic slouched down into a defeated stance, but Lauren looked optimistic. "That's true, Nic. With all the kids around, no one"—she glanced over Nic's shoulder toward Mark—"will get the wrong idea."

"People get the wrong idea all the time, Lauren." Something in her tone of voice must have alerted her sister because she saw the telltale worry lines between her perfectly plucked eyebrows. Nic sorted through her options, all of which were awful. Sharing a room with Mark was just the most recent awfulness in a string of trouble this week. She had survived the rest; she could survive this too. And it beat sleeping in a rest-area parking lot.

As she was trying to come to terms with her situation, her sister's expression was growing more concerned. She had to play it cool. "You're right, it'll work out. Besides, it's just for a few days, and I know we'll be busy." Hopefully too busy to think.

At the sound of a knock, Lauren opened the door, revealing a man and three children, the latter all boys, all wearing swimsuits. The man said, "Hi, Lauren." He saw Nic and nodded. "Nicole, hello. Mark said you'd be here, thanks for coming." Nic recognized Mark's oldest brother, Jim. He looked a little uncomfortable talking with her, but that was to be expected.

"Hey, Jim!" Mark called. At the sound of his voice all three boys came screaming into the room, nearly knocking Nic over, and all three managed to step on at least one of her bags. "Marky! Marky!" they cried. "You came!"

"Of course. I wouldn't miss seeing you guys for the world. Are you ready for"—he crouched down, hands up, eyes wide with drama—"the slide of doom?"

Over the screaming from the kids Nic could barely make out Jim saying to Mark, "I'm so sorry about this. I know the babysitting time hasn't started yet. Meredith is off with her sister and I still have to unpack, and they are just crazy to get in the pool. Is there any way you can take them now?"

Mark walked between Nic and her sister as if they weren't there. As his arm brushed hers, Nic backed out of his way and watched as he took the pile of towels Jim was offering and gave him a one-armed, back-thumping hug. "Of course it's okay! It's good to see you."

The tallest of the boys was standing next to Mark, mimicking the way he hung his right thumb in the pocket of his canvas pants. The other two boys grabbed hold of the back of Mark's belt and tried to climb him. Or were they just gleefully kicking him? Nic grabbed her bags by the shoulder straps and dragged them to the wall, out of harm's way.

"Well, we miss having you over. And not just because you kept the boys entertained."

"Marky," said the oldest boy, "I have a pellet gun." Mark immediately threw his hands up in the air and cried out, and the boy laughed and said, "You didn't do anything wrong! Besides, I don't have it here. Mom said I couldn't bring it."

Nic backed away as the others talked. After all, the Vang family wasn't her family. At least Lauren was here. But being the sister of someone who had married a Vang didn't make her family, it made her a reasonably trustworthy babysitter. And from the look of things, it also made her second in command at best. She could see one of two scenarios working out: either she would be ordered around like a maid, or she would be ignored and paid to do nothing at all. The second option would be okay if she hadn't had her fill of feeling incompetent over the last couple days.

Nic caught Lauren's eye. "I'm going to get the rest of my stuff," she said.

"I'll help you," Lauren offered.

"No. Thank you."

Jim backed out the door ahead of them, thanking Mark again, and Nic and Lauren followed. That left Mark alone with the kids, and the sound of their hollering and wrestling followed them down the hall as they made their way to the elevator. "I can get it myself, in one trip," Nic said softly to her sister. For that, she got the ever-so-tiny head shake. The "don't argue in front of Jim" meaning was implicit. But Nic couldn't let her big sister see her car. At least not yet.

Jim walked past the elevator, probably heading back to his room, Nic thought. Once the doors slid shut, Nic turned to her sister and said, "You should have told me he was going to be working too. I figured I'd see him here and there, but not like this."

"When Lisa and Jeff canceled at the last minute, Chris asked him to come. But Chris said Mark had other plans for the holiday. So I asked you to come." The elevator came to a slow stop. "I tried to let you know, Nic. When I called, your phone went straight to voicemail."

Nic had left the charger at the house, and she hadn't replaced it yet. "My phone's dead."

"I suppose you don't have to stay if you don't want to," Lauren said. "I know how great you are with kids. And Mark is... well, Mark is Mark. I don't have to tell you how unreliable he can be."

Mark was a goofball. He was everyone's favorite uncle

and cousin, so he was naturally perfect for this babysitting job. Besides, Lauren had once been Mark's biggest promoter, at least where Nic was concerned. But as she watched her sister slowly shake her head, arms crossed, eyebrows drawn, Nic realized that had changed, and something more than the obvious—the fact that Mark had broken up with her a year ago—had changed it. She resisted the urge to ask why Lauren was so negative about her new brother-in-law. Mark's life wasn't any of her business.

Besides, Lauren had leveled the same criticism against Nic in the past. And she probably would again.

The elevator doors opened to show a family of five. The adults greeted Lauren, and Nic heard the note of relief in their voices. Their three kids ran in circles around their mom's legs. Nic guessed the dad was a Vang —he had thick, wavy brown hair with just a hint of bronze, the same as Mark. She was pretty sure all the Vang men did.

Lauren introduced Nic, but they didn't seem to care one way or the other who Nic was, only that someone would be taking the kids to the pool. If she had to guess, it had been a long, loud day in the car for this family. Lauren asked if they'd read the parent instruction sheet—they hadn't—but lucky for them, she had several spares in her purse. As she sorted through her bag, Nic made a break for it. She walked fast through the lobby, out across the spacious front porch, and down the steps. That was when the ten-degree morning took the air out of her lungs. But she had to make a good head start. Once she figured she was out of sight, she jogged across the parking lot, the lug soles of her leather boots squeaking on the fresh snow.

Nic had parked her old Subaru at the far end of the lot under the slim shelter of a dormant cottonwood tree. She might have pulled into an employee parking space, but no one had complained yet. She grabbed her guitar case and a big, soft-sided bag printed with a gaudy purple floral pattern. Elliot and Petra called it the Boredom Bag because it was meant to cure boredom.

Just thinking about them stopped her in her tracks. Would the new nanny remember Elliot's applesauce for long car trips? And what about Petra's ribbon collection? Who would bring her colorful new strips to braid?

The crunch of approaching footsteps made her heart jump. Nic glanced behind her. Lauren was coming, wearing her silk blouse and trousers without a coat, and making good time even though she was skidding on her slick, dressy shoes. Nic locked and shut the Subaru's door and walked toward Lauren as fast as she could without arousing any suspicion. As soon as they met, Lauren looked over Nic's shoulder at the dingy little green car. "I can carry more," she said.

"I got it all, thanks."

Lauren frowned. "Why is your car so full of stuff?"

"Besides ski gear, I have things in there that need to be donated." Nic was surprised how smoothly the words slipped out of her mouth, but she knew better than to think her sister would be satisfied. Nic started walking briskly toward the resort, and Lauren had no choice but to follow.

Ahead, the front entrance beckoned, and to her left Nic saw a cloud of steam rising from the hot-spring pool. From what she'd read online, the main building was about a century old. It had been a sanitarium once, a haven for tuberculosis patients with its hot springs and clean mountain air. But now the air felt icy, sharp, and thin. She pulled the mitten hood of her fingerless yellow gloves over her fingers and then placed her hand over her face to warm the air coming into her lungs.

"So how's work going?" Lauren said as she came up beside her.

Lauren's radar was functioning well, as usual. "I love my job," Nic said. It was all she could manage. Lauren didn't have time to pry, because as soon as they passed through the front doors, an older woman called out, "There you are! I have a question for you, Lauren."

There was no mistaking the woman. Nic had mostly seen her in passing and had managed to avoid her at Lauren's wedding, but more than a year ago Mrs. Vang had invited Nic and Mark to dinner at her house. "You'll love her when you get to know her," Mark had said. Nic had been a queasy, nervous mess, and she hadn't put in a good showing. Thankfully a blizzard had given her and Mark an excuse to leave early.

From what she'd heard, mostly from Lauren, Mrs. Vang was meticulous and quite possibly omniscient. She was Jim, Chris, and Mark's mom, and now she was Lauren's mother-in-law too. With her black-and-gray hair and her strong features, she looked fierce and even beautiful—in a Morticia Addams sort of way.

Given a choice between chatting with Lauren and Mrs. Vang or seeing Mark again up in her room, Nic couldn't decide which fate was more terrible. But when she realized Mark was probably busy in the pool by now and she might have the suite to herself, she decided to make for the stairs. She shifted some things to her right hand, then reached out with her left to take the guitar case. Lauren was distracted, and it slipped out of her hand. Nic crept away as the first barrage of questions—something about room assignments and motion sickness—hit Lauren.

She gave Lauren one last look before turning the corner. Her sister had her stone angel face on, emanating cool peacefulness. That meant she was feeling overwhelmed, or irate, but Mrs. Vang didn't know that. Lauren might just be a fair match for Mrs. Vang.

The stairs were empty. Even the hall was empty. And when Nic slipped in the key card and opened the door, she discovered the hotel suite was empty.

There were three doors at the other end of the room. She tried the one on the right first. It led to a big room with one window. In the middle of the bed's lofty blue comforter was a familiar suitcase, and on top of that, a big olive-drab parka with neon green zippers.

She walked in slowly and picked it up. The cuffs were frayed now. She found the patch on the side, under the arm, where the barbed wire had snagged the nylon canvas. A hint of scent reached her—balsam and all things woodsy and comforting. She ran her fingers along the front of the shoulder, where she'd leaned so often. Then Nic set the jacket back down, arranging it to look something like she'd seen it at first, and left the room.

They would be sharing a bathroom, and her bedroom was to the left. It was smaller than his, but comfortable, with an old brass bed and at least a dozen pillows. It looked more feminine than Mark's room. The pale yellow on the walls reminded her of her grandmother's house. Nic looked at the bed's inviting softness, the winter-white flannel duvet over a downy comforter and pillows she could tunnel beneath. It wasn't ten o'clock yet, so she couldn't give in to her urge, but she would. Not a moment before then. And now wasn't the time for tears. It was time to make money and make Christmas memories for some young kids. Best of all, she had a decent and free place to sleep for a couple nights.

So what if Mark was here? It wasn't the worst thing that had happened to her this week. He and his forest-smelling jacket could jump in a lake. "Men stink," she said aloud, and then smiled at her own joke. Sure, sometimes it was a nice stink. She just needed to get her hands on a bar of whatever soap he used, tuck it into her pillowcase, and she'd never have a reason to miss him again.

She moved all of her things into her room, took off her gray wool coat, and checked her face in the mirror. She saw the same shiny, dark brown hair skimming her shoulders and the same gray eyes. Her girlfriends at school said they were jealous of her large eyes. The boys at school called her bug-eyed. Nic's opinion was somewhere in between.

Her brown eyeliner hadn't smudged, and there was still a little sparkle of champagne-colored shadow on her eyelids. Of course, the pool would erase all of that. But right now she looked like she usually did, and that was better than she'd expected. All the more reason to wait until ten o'clock to think about the things she didn't want to think about.

She found the schedule Lauren had emailed her. Pool time didn't officially start until after lunch. She had fished her phone out of the duffel bag and taken it to the couch, settling in with it to read chapter three of a good e-book on her phone, when she heard the door buzz, click, and open.

She was certain it was going to be Lauren, but it wasn't. It was Mark, shirtless and wearing a ridiculously huge pair of orange swim shorts with a white towel draped over his head like the ugliest bridal veil in the universe. It was covering his eyes, so he tipped his head back to get a look at her. "Hey," he said.

She gave him a perfunctory smile and looked back at her phone screen. Her neck felt as if a blush was blooming there. She'd better get herself under control or she'd never make it through Christmas.

He scrubbed his hair with the towel and wandered toward her, dripping all the way. Then he tossed the wet towel onto a chair and sat down on it.

Men are unbelievably annoying, she thought.

She didn't look up. From her one quick glance, it looked as if he had grown some real chest hair. She so wanted to look, but just the thought of it made the heat on her neck creep upward. How long had it been since she'd seen him without a shirt? More than a year ago? Probably that time he asked her to come along on a youth group trip to the indoor water park. When was that?

She forced herself to read the words on the screen. The heroine, a spunky young woman on the western frontier, was trying to sort out her physical reaction to the mysterious ranch hand, and it made Nic want to toss her phone across the room. Stupid woman, she thought, get on with your life. If he loves you, he'll make it work. If he doesn't, he'll break up with you on Christmas Eve, talk to you once, and then, at his brother's wedding a week later, talk for five minutes and avoid you the rest of the night. And there's not a thing you can do to change it.

"Reading a book?" Mark asked.

"Trying to," she said. She tucked her chin down into the cowl of her oversized sweater.

"Meredith found out Jim gave the kids to me early, and that was the end of that. She said he needs more time alone with the kids or else he'll never truly appreciate her job as a mom." He laughed.

Nic didn't find that funny at all. It made perfect sense to her.

"So," he continued, "we'll have lunch in about twenty minutes."

"Yes," she said. So put some clothes on, she thought.

"Mom wants us to sit with her."

Nic looked up at him. She hoped he was teasing her, but she could tell he was in earnest.

"You know, just to get to know you," he added.

"Why would she want to get to know me?" Nic said. When they were dating, Nic was never invited along to Mark's family home, or on his parents' rare visits to see him. Except for that disastrous Thanksgiving. Now they weren't dating, and suddenly the woman wanted to get to know her? It was more likely that Mrs. Vang wanted to personally interview her before letting her near the brood of grandchildren. Nic resisted the urge to get up and check her clothes and makeup. Mrs. Vang and everyone else in the world were going to think whatever they wanted about her, and there was precious little she could do about it.

She felt a twinge in her heart. It would be good to have someone on her side. Her sister cared very much, in her bossy, nosy way. But this new disaster in her life… there was no telling how Lauren would react to that.

"I guess I'd better get changed," he said, standing up—and leaving the wet towel on the chair. She tried not to look at it. She tried not to let it drive her insane that it was soaking into the upholstery. But after he disappeared into his room, she put her phone down with a sigh. She'd have to move it.

Just then he jogged back out and snatched up the towel. "Sorry," he said, grinning at her. He'd probably done that on purpose, just to tease her. She could have sworn she heard him chuckle when he got back into his room. But rather than feeling mad, tears stung her eyes. Not now, she thought. Not yet.

After deciding that walking into the restaurant with him would feel awkward, she went down to the lobby while he was still changing. She took a moment to admire the hotel's old architecture, the high ceilings and the painted white wooden beams, and the soft dove color of the walls. The windows to the left of the front doors spanned from floor to ceiling, containing dozens of small panes, many of which had the wavy look of old glass. The lobby's floor was wood and looked well worn, but it was smooth and glossy. There was a new granite top at the front desk, an elaborate antler chandelier in the sitting area, and a huge moose head mounted on the wall above her. Everything was decorated for Christmas, but the moose head would have looked a lot better decorating a moose body, she thought.

"Nicole Benedict," a woman said. Nic turned to see Mrs. Vang walking up to her. "Do you mind joining me at my table for lunch?"

"Thank you," she said. She felt as if she were being summoned to the high table in a medieval novel and she should have curtsied. And being summoned to the high table never went well for the heroine in the books she read. Unless the prince rescued her, of course. She reminded herself this was just a person, just a lunch. Although the family was well-known, there would be no princes at the Vang Christmas family retreat.

Mrs. Vang strolled into the restaurant, and Nic followed. Walking behind Mrs. Vang—her flowing hand-knit sweater and her high heels—made Nic feel like a child. She waited to be motioned toward a chair and then sat at a table in the wide bay window, her back to the rest of the tables. Mrs. Vang sat opposite her. She raised one hand, her bracelets clinking together, and waved someone over. Soon after, her husband appeared, a small plate of goodies in one hand and a glass of red wine in the other. He smiled at Nic, wrinkles fanning out around his eyes, then sat down to her right, his concentration falling to the olives on his plate.

The last chair moved and Nic turned to see Mark plop down into it, wearing a pair of jeans and a hoodie. "Hey, Mom, how's it going?"

"Well," she said. "Your hair is wet."

He reached up with both hands and tousled it. "Really? How did that happen?"

Quick as lightning, his mother twisted her cloth napkin and snapped it toward him, low and out of sight of the rest of the restaurant. He jerked his knee out of the way in time and laughed.

And Mrs. Vang grinned.

Nic swallowed. She didn't know Mrs. Vang had a

playful side. And she was certain Lauren didn't know either. She took a drink of water and looked away, feeling as if she'd intruded on a private moment.

"So are you ready for the herd of rug rats?" Mr. Vang asked.

It wasn't Nic's favorite way to refer to kids, but he said it with such a glint in his eye she had to smile back. "I am. I really like hanging out with kids. Well, not hanging out, really, but nanny-ing. I mean babysitting." She stopped there, sure that if she spoke any longer she'd only sound more stupid. She took another drink of water.

"I understand you are a professional nanny," Mrs. Vang said.

The water went down wrong. Nic tried not to cough loudly and instead smiled and nodded, unable to breathe. Holding it in just made things worse. After a few seconds she was coughing and tears were pouring out of her eyes. Mark thumped her on her back with his palm, and Mrs. Vang looked seriously concerned. "Excuse me," Nic said as soon as she was able. A waiter filled her water glass and she waited to say thank you, then she said to Mrs. Vang, "I've worked as a nanny in Missoula for almost a year."

"With the same family? Who?"

Nic cleared her throat again. "The Gordons."

"Tim and Marie? He's a deacon at that big church. Bob, what's the name of the one that looks like a hockey arena?"

"That's the one," Nic said, trying to smile. Her lips quivered when she did, so she let it drop. What were the chances Mrs. Vang would know Tim Gordon? Of course she'd probably be on the phone after lunch to check up on her. And then Nic would be looking for a new place to stay the night.

Mark was staring at her. She didn't have to look to know it, she could feel it. All this time and her radar still seemed tuned to him. "Have you seen the new church in Helena, Mom?" he said. "Not so much hockey arena as Colosseum."

Nic wondered if he'd changed the topic on purpose. But that didn't seem likely. She and Mark weren't exactly on the same team anymore.

Mrs. Vang threw her hands up in the air. "That's being generous. I've heard the inside is nothing but a maze of offices. For a church that preaches community service, I can't imagine what business they're doing there that requires all that room."

"Maybe they're vampires," Mr. Vang offered, and Mark laughed.

"These are our brothers and sisters in Christ you're talking about," Mrs. Vang said.

"Then they shouldn't be sucking people's blood," Mr. Vang said, terribly deadpan. Mark laughed again.

For a few minutes father and son exchanged ideas for a name for the new church, all of which seemed terribly off-color to Nic, though a few made her bite her lip to keep from smiling. Mrs. Vang took the teasing well, as if she'd heard it all before.

A waitress appeared beside Nic, and she looked to Mrs. Vang before speaking. "Have you decided, Mrs. Vang?" she asked.

Nic hadn't even looked at the menu.

"We have. Nicole, do you need a moment?" Mrs. Vang asked when she saw Nic pick up the menu.

"I'll only need a second," Nic said. But all she could see were the prices, which were beyond her budget. Was she buying? Was Mrs. Vang? She hadn't even brought a wallet —how foolish was that? She'd have to make a run for the hotel room. She tried to find something that wouldn't be expensive but wouldn't be an obvious attempt not to buy something expensive, either.

Mrs. Vang ordered. Then Mr. Vang. It was Nic's turn. And at that moment Mark leaned her way and touched his finger to one item.

"The Alhambra BLT," Nic said. Her favorite kind of sandwich. He'd remembered.

"I'll have the same," Mark said. "Extra bacon, please."

"Yes, Mr. Vang," the server said, and she gathered up the menus.

The waitress knew him? *Mr. Vang.* It was hard to think of him with that title, but as she looked at him now, it fit. She wondered if something had changed. She had always thought of him as young, somewhere between a boy and a young adult. That just didn't seem to fit right now, despite the way he teased and joked. He looked comfortable in his own skin, she thought. Confident. She didn't remember seeing that before.

How would the Vang family describe her? she wondered. Had she moved on from young woman to woman in their eyes? Nic reviewed her lunchtime performance so far, and doubted it.

She experienced a reprieve for a while as Mark asked his mother about the health and welfare of various family members and neighbors, and thankfully the food arrived quickly. It was the fanciest toasted BLT she'd ever seen, and it smelled delicious. She thanked the server, and

Mark reached for her hand. It startled her so much she faltered before realizing Mark's father's hand was waiting as well. Mark wasn't trying to be affectionate, he was trying to say grace, and they were waiting on her. Bob said a short grace, but Nic didn't hear a word of it. All she could think about was how warm Mark's hand was. It always had been, just as certainly as hers was usually cold. He gave her a quick squeeze and then drew it away. Her hand felt colder in his absence.

"Lauren says you're studying classical guitar," Mrs. Vang said, and just like that Nic's appetite vanished. Another horrible topic. But that wasn't Mrs. Vang's fault, it was Nic's. Her entire life had been a series of horrible choices. She could lie, but not only was that wrong, she was a terrible liar. All she could do was lay it out for them, and her ex-boyfriend, to see.

"I was, but I didn't go back to school for my sophomore year," she said. "My plan was to save up some money by working all year." That wasn't exactly a lie. Well, it was, but it was the same lie she chose to tell herself—that she'd be back in school soon. Maybe. "The Gordons are very busy people, so I moved into their house and took on some additional duties."

"I see," Mrs. Vang said, for all the world looking as if she could see right through her.

Nic's face grew hot. Did her words sound inappropriate? Would a sensible person, a nanny, have refused to move in with the family? She couldn't think about that now. She couldn't think about the kids, or him. She glanced at Mark, hoping he had something funny and distracting to say, but he was staring at her right hand. She followed his gaze and saw the fork quivering in her grip. She set it down, a little too loudly, and tucked her hands into her lap.

"How many children do they have?" Mrs. Vang asked.

"Two. Petra and Elliot. Petra is nine, and she's very into the job of big sister." Nic grinned. "Elliot does well on his end too, playing the annoying little brother. They really love each other. Sure they get on each other's nerves, but I've never seen a brother and sister so close."

"That says something about your influence," Mrs. Vang said. "Fostering love between siblings is an important job."

"I agree. I think it's hard not to compare them to each other in a way that brings out a competitive streak. And at the same time, a little competition is important. Just the other day Elliot—"

The memory came to her mind clearly, and at the same time she felt grief strike her like a kick to the chest. She was never going to see them again. Did they think she'd abandoned them? Did they doubt she'd ever loved them? What had *he* told them about her?

"Excuse me," she said, feigning the return of her cough, and she stood up so fast that she shifted the tablecloth and all the water glasses sloshed. She headed out into the lobby, past tables full of Vangs and people who looked as if they should be. It was a thing of mercy that she saw the "Restrooms" sign. She dove inside and hid in a stall, standing, her hands pressed to her temples. Not now, she thought over and over. Not now. It wasn't time to cry yet. She only had—she calculated—seven and a half hours to go. The tears came anyway, and she covered her mouth with her sweater sleeves to keep herself silent. But the restroom was empty and every gasping breath echoed on the white tile walls.

She wrestled herself for control, then emerged to wipe her face with a cool, wet paper towel. But in the mirror her pale skin looked splotchy and the whites of her eyes were red, making the irises of her gray eyes look green and glassy. Mark called it her stormy-seas look, and told her it was "just another kind of beautiful." If he thought she looked beautiful last Christmas Eve when he broke up with her, he hadn't said a word about it.

Nic fanned her face for a bit and then forced a big smile. That helped a little. Mrs. Vang was just a woman, this was just a job, and it would all be over soon enough. She walked back to the table as casually as she could manage and found the others happily discussing how much a little girl named Cici had grown and how much she loved her newborn brother.

Nic sat down and glanced around. The other three plates were all nearly empty. How long had she been hiding in the bathroom? She took a couple quick bites of the exotic-looking coleslaw, and that was enough for her rebellious stomach. There was no way she was going to be able to finish. She heard someone walk up beside her, and the server set a to-go food box down beside her plate.

"I know you don't like eating a lot before going swimming," Mark said.

She was about to disagree when she saw an encouraging smile on his face. He was covering for her. "Thank you," she said. She was pretty sure a girl couldn't feel more pathetic than when her ex-boyfriend was feeling sorry for her.

Nic got herself together. She asked Mrs. Vang about her gorgeous sweater jacket, learned a little about the artist that made it, and complimented her on her good taste. And she talked olives with Mr. Vang, sharing her favorite brand of Greek olives—not too much oil or garlic, plenty of vinegary tartness, and a hint of red pepper. She packed up her sandwich when Mark noted the time. Agreeing that people should be dropping the kids by at any moment, she finally made her escape.

As they walked out of the restaurant Mark said, "That was fun."

Nic bit back a sharp response and chose to say nothing.

They both turned toward the stairs rather than the elevator and started the trek up toward the suite.

"You wanna talk?" Mark asked.

"No." A thousand times no, she thought. She had wanted to be better employed, and maybe even engaged, the next time she saw him. She hadn't even wanted to be a nanny anymore. How ironic, now that she would do anything to keep her job. Well, not anything. That was the problem.

Mark was frowning at her. "The wheels are turning so hard in there I feel like I should spray some WD-40 in your ear before you lock up."

"Ha." As they entered the second-floor hall, she saw a family already knocking at the door of their suite. It was the same family she'd seen near the elevator with Lauren, and again all three kids were running circles around their mom's legs. This time the oldest girl, who looked to be about nine, was yelling "Stop it!" at the other two as she ran after them. Dad was rubbing the bridge of his nose between his thumb and forefinger, and the mom knocked a little louder.

"Ella-Eva-Eddie! What are you doing?" Mark called.

The kids took one look at him and ran down the hall at full speed. Mark opened his arms wide and managed each collision in turn, from oldest to youngest. That last one was a little boy hovering somewhere between toddler and school age.

"Marky! Marky!" the little boy yelled. It seemed to be the official Mark greeting. Both of the little girls were talking at the same time about the puppy their parents didn't let them have, the mean boy next door, and more.

Nic stepped past them and shook hands with the parents. "I'm Nicole, Lauren's sister," she said.

"Oh, that's right, you're helping Mark," the dad said. "Glad to meet you."

"This is my husband, Edward Vang. Mark's cousin. I'm Ingrid—Eddie, get down off of Mark right now."

Ingrid walked past Nic, her husband followed, and their short conversation was over. With an inward shrug, Nic pulled out her key card and entered the room, deciding she might as well change.

She put on a pair of cute turquoise-colored board shorts and a plain white bikini top and covered that with a short-sleeved rash-guard shirt. She'd learned over the last year that there was nothing to be gained by trying to tug down or pull up a bathing suit while managing kids in a pool. Besides, grasping little swimmers could dislodge even the most sporty one-piece suit. She was about to step out into the living room when she halted. She was wearing shorts and a T-shirt. Why did she suddenly feel like she needed a cover-up?

How many times had she worn just this sort of outfit in front of *him,* walking to and from the Gordons' backyard pool? Maybe it was different because it was a bathing suit. Maybe no woman should be walking around in a bathing suit in front of a married man. In his home.

She shook her head. Second-guessing wasn't going to help her. She'd always been a modest dresser, and she didn't think that was the problem. She'd been uncomfortable from time to time, but there hadn't been any real clues, had there? Had she given signals she hadn't meant to send?

She opened the door to find eight little kids climbing all over Mark, who was flat on the floor. He raised one hand to wave goodbye as Ingrid and Edward left. Ella, Eva, Eddie—she could spot their very blond heads. And three more boys had arrived, the ones she'd met earlier, including the gun-toting oldest one. That left one child unidentified, a very little girl who was tugging on Mark's ear and giggling. Cici, maybe?

At the sound of another knock, Nic maneuvered around the melee and opened the door. Outside stood a woman and a little girl, the girl pressing her face into her mother's skirt, clutching her for comfort. The mom looked up for a moment.

Sad, Nic thought. Something in her eyes made Nic's heart go out to her.

"Hi, I'm Tracie Vang." The woman quickly looked back to her child. "It'll be fun, Melly," she said. She didn't sound convinced herself.

Nic got down to the girl's level. "Hi, my name is Nic. I've never been here before, have you?"

The girl was still. Not even the light brown curls on her head moved.

"I heard the swimming pool is super fun and warm. I like being warm. I like swimming too. Do you?"

The girl nodded, but she kept her grip on her mother's skirt.

"Do you want to go with me?"

The girl shook her head.

Nic grew conscious of all the laughter and yelling behind her. "Those kids sound crazy, huh? Wanna know who the craziest one is? His name is Mark. Do you know him?"

The girl peeked over her shoulder. "Mark?"

"I told you he'd be here, Melly," her mother said. "You're going to have so much fun." Again the hint of doubt.

"Yup, your mom's right. Want to say hi to Mark?"

Before the girl could decide, Mark came toward them wearing kids like a drowning man might wear seaweed. "Melly girl! You made it!" She gave him a shy smile but didn't let go of her mom. That didn't deter him. Mark grabbed her and lifted her up above the crowd, depositing her on his shoulders. She giggled. Then he leaned over Ella and Eva and gave Melly's mom a one-armed hug, holding on to her daughter's leg with his other hand. "I'm so glad you made it, Tracie."

"Yeah, well. Our plans changed."

The woman had seemed older at first, but once Nic had a chance to take a better look at her, she decided they might be the same age, in their early twenties. Tracie didn't look like a Vang with her blue eyes, freckles, and strawberry-blond hair. Melly's curly brown hair and big blue eyes looked just like a Vang. Tracie must have married one of Mark's cousins or uncles or some other member of the clan. But where was he?

"What happened?" Mark asked.

"I talked to Cole about our plans for Christmas yesterday. I don't know if he forgot or something else came up." Tracie's eyes darted up to her daughter's face. Melly was busy waving at the kids below her. "He won't be in town. I guess that's no surprise," she said. The woman seemed to age again.

"I'm sorry, Tracie," he said. "I was praying things would turn out differently."

Nic looked at Tracie's left hand. No ring. Something about the conversation made her think Tracie was divorced. It was just like Mark to come to the rescue.

"Can we swim, Uncle Mark?" Melly said from over his head.

"You betcha, Melly. Can I talk you into going with us, Tracie?" he asked. "I might let you beat me for a lap or two. Before I win."

Tracie wrinkled her nose, which looked adorable. "You wish. Just wait until we get back to our home turf. I've been doing laps with a cute little girl on my back." Then she winked, which looked even more adorable.

Nic felt her face turning red. Tracie and Mark had a relationship. They'd been swimming together, and would be again, and they obviously knew each other well. And above all else, her sweet, curly-haired daughter loved him.

Nic reminded herself again that he had broken up with her. His dating someone else was inevitable. And she was ready to move on too, she just hadn't met the right guy yet. The best thing she could do now, for herself and him, was to wish him well.

"I'm sorry, Nic," he said. He looked as if he'd forgotten she even existed. "This is Tracie Vang. Tracie, this is Nic Benedict."

Tracie glanced at Mark. She grinned. "It's a pleasure to meet you. You must be—"

"She's babysitting with me," Mark said quickly. "Then I guess you're going back to Missoula, right, Nic?"

Now Mark was trying to keep Tracie from thinking there was something more than babysitting going on in the suite, Nic thought. She swallowed and smiled. "That's the plan. I can't wait to get back." Another lie. With practice like this, she might end up being a good liar after all. Lying wasn't any more uncomfortable than having no idea where she would be in three days.

"Oh. I see." Something passed across Tracie's expression. Was it doubt? Surprise?

Nic didn't want to ruin whatever it was that the two of them had going on. It wasn't her place. "I'd better round everyone up," she said. A moment later the door was shut and Tracie was gone, and Mark deposited Melly on a chair. "Wait a second," he said dramatically. "Is everyone ready to go swimming? I see you have your suit on. Eddie, that's an excellent towel. Spectacular floaties, Miss Cici." He jogged over to the kitchen countertop, leaping over one of the boys as he did, grabbed a set of goggles, and put them on. "I'm all ready to go too!"

The short crowd giggled and a few of them cried, "No!"

"What, did I forget something?"

"Yes!" they yelled.

"No, I didn't, I—wait, what? What happened to my bathing suit?"

The appreciative crowd hooted.

"Give me one second and I'll change," he said. He disappeared into his bedroom.

Silence descended on the room, and Nic turned around slowly. Eight sets of eyes focused on her, with expressions that ranged from disappointed to frightened. And Nic was at a loss for words.

They can smell your fear, she thought. She had to move fast. "I know, it's time for me to learn your names."

"Mark already knows our names," an older boy muttered.

"Well, I know your name too," she said, and for some reason, her mind settled on Mr. Vang. "It's Grampa Bob."

A couple of the kids tittered. "It is not Grampa Bob, it's Tegan," the boy said.

"Tegan? Rats, I was sure it was Bob! But that's okay. At least I know your name." She pointed at one of the two girls that made up Ella-Eva-Eddie. "Your name is Bob." Everyone but Tegan giggled.

“No, you silly goose, it’s Ella,” she said. “I’m not a boy. Bob is a boy’s name,” she added with enough sass to rival any teenager.

Now she had Ella, Eva, and Eddie straight. After two more “Bobs” everyone had offered up their name, and she’d earned a few more giggles as well. “Okay, the guy in there,” she said, pointing toward Mark’s door, “That’s…”

“That’s not Bob!” Eva said.

“That’s Mark,” a few others offered. Just like magic the door opened, and the kids swarmed him as if he’d been gone for months. Any appreciation she might have gained paled in his spotlight.

Mark led the kids out the door, and they followed loudly. Even Melly left her quiet spot on the chair to trail him, although she lagged behind the others. At the top of the stairs, Melly held out her hand, and without hesitation

Nic took it in her own. They walked down together, and at the bottom of the stairs Melly let go and jogged after the others without ever having looked up at Nic.

Nic was pretty sure that Edward and Ingrid, the parents of the E-kids, were right. She was going to be Mark's assistant this weekend. The kids made a break for the indoor pool, and they burst into the echoing solitude of a few adult swimmers. The indoor pool was beautiful and peaceful, with cobalt-blue tile all around, a full wall of windows revealing the twin outdoor pool beyond, and skylights above. But the kids' voices reverberated through the airy space, and when Mark suggested they all go outside, Nic couldn't have agreed more.

While snow was everywhere, the outdoor pool was a misty haven of warmth. The three brothers ran and jumped, including the very young Sebastian, and disappeared into the steam. Mark had to hurry to catch up with them. Ella and Eva complained about the sulfur smell of the hot spring, but they dipped their feet into the warm water, and Eddie walked down the steps beside them. Melly and the littlest girl, Cici, stayed back from the edge. The cold air swirled with the warm steam around them, and Nic felt the chill.

It took a little cajoling, but Nic was able to convince the two girls that she was their boat and all they had to do was climb on. Pretty soon she was tugging Eddie, Melly, and Cici around in the shallows, making motorboat noises. Ella and Eva watched, but they had their own games to play. They had excellent swimming skills, but Nic kept an eye on them.

All the while she could hear the kids on the other side of the pool get louder and louder, and through the mist she spotted arcs of water and flailing arms, sure signs of epic water fights taking place. Ella and Eva defected to the other side, and Nic followed, with the little ones tight as ticks on her arms and back. All three could swim with or without her, so she wasn't surprised when Sebastian jumped into the fray with his big brothers.

As soon as she swam closer to Mark and the other kids, Nic became a home base of sorts. They hid behind her or hung off her shoulders to catch their breath. Then they attacked Mark with loud, if poorly aimed, splashes.

Mark obliged them with dramatic defeats that ended every time with a spectacular capsize into the water. In the silence that followed, kids giggled and squealed, knowing that one of them was going to feel a tug on the ankle at any moment.

Nic couldn't help but notice how clever Mark was with the kids or how gentle he could be with the littler ones. Or how long and lean his arms were cutting through the water. She'd lost some of her muscle tone since the days when he and she had made time for hiking or biking or even climbing at the gym. And walking. So many long walks, talking, or even singing as they walked. How could she forget?

Mark caught her staring at him and smiled broadly. She looked away. After that, Nic kept her attention on the kids.

After a long time swimming, the littlest ones started shivering. Nic guessed it was probably from fatigue as much as the cold. She rounded up Melly, Cici, Sebastian, and Eddie, all of whom had slightly blue lips, and marched them back up to the room. She had them all stand together in their colorful swimsuits under the shower to get the chlorine off. She drummed on the sink to make thunder noises for their rain shower. The kids thought she was hilarious, mostly, she thought, because there was no Mark around for comparison.

After that, she wrapped the whole crew in fresh towels and sat them down on the couch. She had animal crackers in the Boredom Bag, of course, and a Winnie-the-Pooh book, but they were restless. Sebastian accused Eddie of hogging the couch, and Melly looked so tired she could cry.

The moment called for a guitar. Nic made a dash for her room and parted the kids, sitting down in the damp middle of the couch where they could touch the guitar. But only gently, she reminded them.

She picked a fun song first, a children's song about swimming. The bigger ones got the jokes, and Melly was just happy to drum softly on the end of the guitar. Cici stared at the silver tuning keys as if they were sparkly Christmas ornaments. Having gotten their attention, Nic switched to a lullaby. Just as she thought they would, they all slouched down in the sleepy, soft way that only kids could do. By the next song, Eddie had closed his eyes.

When the others arrived, the peaceful moment dissolved into chaos. For the next half hour, she and Mark got the rest of the kids showered, fed everyone most of her BLT sandwich and half of her animal cracker supply, and soothed more than a couple tiredness-induced breakdowns. When the first knock came at 5:30, the kids were miraculously quiet. No one was crying or hitting anyone else, and to the parents who had been enjoying the family meet-and-greet down in the pub, Nic thought, she and Mark must have looked like geniuses. In one towel-covered parade, all the kids left at once.

It was time to change for dinner, but Nic was exhausted. She missed Petra and Elliot. A lot. By now she'd be making their favorite Friday meal, along with popcorn for movie night, because Fridays were a social night for the Gordons. Did they have a new nanny already? Would she know that Elliot liked sea salt and Petra liked a little coconut oil with the butter?

Mark was leaning back against the kitchen sink, downing his second large glass of water. When the glass tipped up just so, she could sneak another peek at his strong shoulders.

"Do you want to jump in the shower first?" he said.

Nic was startled. The result of a guilty conscience, no doubt. "Yes, thank you." She was so flustered that she went into the shower without getting a change of clothes. Thankfully he wasn't around when she sneaked back into her room to get dressed again. She towel-dried her hair and put on a hint of makeup, ready to go again. She checked Lauren's schedule and wandered out into the main room.

Nic thought she might take off without Mark, just to make it clear to everyone—including herself—that they weren't a couple. She hoped her meals with Mrs. and Mr. Vang were over, but who should she dine with? Would it be unforgivably rude to dine alone with the book she had loaded onto her phone? She wondered how she was going to manage to make it through the evening.

"Do we have the kids again tonight?" Mark asked from his doorway. He wore jeans and a shirt he hadn't yet buttoned and was rubbing his hair mercilessly with a towel.

She looked away. Did he always have to look so good in everything he did or did not wear? It was one thing to get your heart broken, another entirely to find out that after a year had passed, none of the spark was gone. In fact, it felt worse. More distracting.

But that was only her view of things. As for Mark, he seemed to have moved on—with Tracie. "I don't think so," she said.

"What's on the schedule?"

"It says there's a craft fair in Alhambra tonight, and it looks like everyone is going. But I bet some of the kids would rather be sleeping."

"True. If their parents were hoping we'd tire them out, I think we exceeded their expectations."

"Although you know how it goes, once they've refueled."

"They may not eat after all those animal crackers. It's pretty cool that you had goodies in your diaper bag."

She threw a nasty look his way. "It's so much cooler than just a diaper bag. Although I do have a diaper, if you need one."

He chuckled and ducked back into his room. "We're supposed to have dinner with Chris and Lauren, by the way," he called. "Lauren phoned while you were in the shower."

Nic collapsed onto the couch. She'd rather hug a porcupine. The memory of the disastrous lunch came rushing back, and she decided she'd rather not eat with anyone. "I'm going to do takeout," she said.

Mark popped back out, hair combed and shirt

buttoned, a sweater in his hand. "What?" He strode her way and sat down beside her, giving her a very serious look. "You wouldn't send me in there alone. You're a much nicer person than that."

"Humph. People change."

His eyes glittered and he gave her a mischievous grin. "Not too much, I hope."

She glared at him, resenting how cute he looked, and weighed her options. If she stayed in the room, her sister would grow suspicious and hunt her down. If she went with Mark, Lauren would ask questions, get suspicious, and hunt her down. "I'll go. Can we make it fast?"

She realized her mistake as soon as she asked. They weren't a team. There was no *we*. But he nodded just the same.

"Absolutely. Besides, Chris has had his knickers in a knot about something since I got here. For all I know they'll be the ones cutting it short." He noticed an animal cookie on the couch beside him and handed it to her. "Want it? No?" He popped it in his mouth.

"That's disgusting. You know the young of our species lick their food before they eat it."

"I'm not afraid," he said, grinning again. He was being adorable. She rolled her eyes.

"If we're going, Mark, and we have to be there at six, we have exactly one minute."

He jumped up, grabbed her hand, and pulled her to her feet. "We'll make better time if we slide down the railing."

He was funny. She'd forgotten just how fun he could be—but fun wasn't enough. She pulled her hand away and followed him out the door.

Lauren and Chris were seated by the time they

arrived, and even better for Nic, they were in a corner away from Mrs. and Mr. Vang. But the silence at the table caught her attention right away. Then she saw it. The stone angel face. Lauren's clear, pale skin, her dark gray eyes, and her beatific grin—like Miss America but with far less sincerity. Something was wrong.

"Glad you two could make it," Lauren said as if they were terribly late. Then again, by Lauren's standards, two or three minutes was late.

Chris looked up at Mark, said, "Hey," and then glanced at Nic and added, "Hi, Nicole." Then he started folding his cloth napkin on top of his plate in silence. Knickers in a knot indeed, Nic thought.

She was about to bolt when Mark pulled out a chair for her and started chatting. "Well, the babysitting seems to be going well," he said, and he went on to regale Chris and Lauren with some of the day's funnier moments. Chris listened in a distracted way. Lauren smiled, but she was sitting bolt upright and barely moving a muscle. Nic kicked her once under the table and questioned her with silently raised eyebrows, but Lauren just gave her that tiny head shake. It was her way of saying "shut up" in the quietest, most polite way.

When Mark stopped talking, a stillness settled over the table. "Are you ready for the kids again tomorrow?" Lauren asked, finally breaking the silence.

"It'll be fun," Nic said. "I guess I thought there'd be more kids."

"There might be. Jim and Chris have some friends joining him tomorrow, right, Chris? I believe they have two kids, but they might be older."

"They are business associates more than friends,"

Chris said. Nic studied her sister's husband as he made a meticulous series of origami folds with his napkin. There was a sharpness to his comment that was unusual. Chris usually had a warmth about him, but she couldn't see any trace of that now.

"That makes sense," Mark agreed. "You guys do like to multitask. But as far as the kids go, the more the merrier."

Two symmetrical little lines showed between Lauren's eyebrows. "Are you certain you can keep that many children safe?" She was looking right at Mark when she asked it.

Before Mark could answer, Chris looked up at her. "I'm sure he can," he answered smoothly. "I believe it's Nic who is used to being around fewer children."

"Nic is used to being around children twenty-four hours a day, under all sorts of circumstances," Lauren replied. "And she has taken courses to be certified as a lifeguard."

"But because of the way you phrased that," Chris said, "I'm guessing she did not finish the course, correct? Half an education can be more dangerous than none—besides being a waste of money."

"How interesting, that you think spending money on education is a waste."

"Wow," Mark said. "Fascinating topic. But maybe we should all pick out an entree while we reflect upon what we should talk about next."

Lauren lifted her menu and sat up straighter, and Chris hovered over his. The couple sat there in silence for a few long minutes, and the tension was enough to make Nic's temples throb.

There was no BLT on the dinner menu. Mark leaned

toward her and whispered, "Ceasar's." She loved a good Ceasar salad. A year had passed, but he still remembered. "And pie."

That made her giggle. She loved pie too. "With cheddar."

"Weirdo."

"You never gave it a fair chance," she said.

"It just covers up the taste of the fruit."

"That's like saying the crust covers up the taste of the fruit. It enhances it. The only thing keeping pie from being a perfect food is that it needs more fat and salt."

"Two of my favorite food groups," Mark said. "But that doesn't mean all delicious foods belong in the same place at the same time. Except in my stomach."

Nic grinned, and so did Mark until a strange look came over his face. She followed his gaze to her sister and brother-in-law. They were looking at their younger siblings with barely concealed irritation.

"Ahem," Nic said. "Well then." She looked back down at her menu.

All was well for a short moment until Mark whispered, "I'm still getting pie." Nic dissolved into giggles.

"Could you be more childish, Mark?" Chris asked his brother.

"Nicole, seriously," Lauren added. "You have real responsibilities here. And this isn't a—a dating service."

"You did not just say that," Nic said. But her sister was getting red in the face, the precursor to tears, which were often followed by an argument or lecture that took entirely too long to complete. "I'm sorry, Lauren. I do take caring for kids seriously, but I might as well have fun while I'm doing it."

"It doesn't end up being fun, does it?" Chris said, pointing his napkin at his brother. "Not if your whole life falls apart because of it."

"O—kay," Mark said softly. "I don't really know what either of you are talking about, but you're both being loud and harsh, and I'm not sure you want everyone in the restaurant to overhear what you're saying."

Chris and Lauren both glanced up and around and apparently didn't like what they saw. Lauren bit her lip and Chris tucked his napkin on his lap.

"May I take your order?" a server said.

Everyone was fairly well behaved after that, although Mark and Nic had to carry most of the conversation as they ate. She knew Mark had left Missoula shortly after they broke up, but she didn't know he'd landed in Glendive. From what he said, the winters there were tough, the thunderstorms were astonishing, and the nearby oil fields had an undeniable effect on the town in good and bad ways.

That was when she noticed the way his eyes lit up when he talked about a certain small church there, and some of the community service projects the teenagers in the church were completing. His voice dropped and he leaned forward onto the table. His hands, which had been flying through the air as he spoke, grasped his elbows. It was a conundrum she'd almost forgotten. When he was the most excited, he grew still. And somewhere in the middle of his story, he mentioned being a custodian.

"What?" Chris asked. "You're a custodian? For the church?"

Mark nodded.

"You're twenty-five years old, you were one semester

away from completing your physical therapist certification, and now you're a janitor?"

Mark returned Chris's gaze, and a slow smile spread across his face. His eyes, however, were dark slits. On those few occasions he got angry, he could be especially still. She'd almost forgotten that too.

"That's right. And since when do you think I should be a PT?" Mark asked.

"Since you spent all that money on it. But you know you should have been a doctor," Chris said.

Mark sat quietly for a moment. He took a deep breath and turned to Nic. "Are you finished?"

"Yup."

They stood up together, and Lauren said softly to Chris, "Now look what you've done."

They started across the restaurant, but then Mark touched her arm and said, "I'll meet you up there." She nodded, hoping he wasn't on his way back to the table to start a fight. But that wasn't his style. She went on without him.

Nic tried to guess what Chris and Lauren were mad about. It seemed as if they were mad about everything. But what was shocking was the way Chris had seemed to aim insults at Nic. He'd always been more than kind to her. Things had been awkward when she and Mark broke up, but that was to be expected. Mark was Chris's brother, after all.

How things had changed. It was Lauren and Chris who had set Nic and Mark up on their first date, a double date with them more than a year ago. Lauren had nothing but glowing things to say about Mark and how perfect he was for her little sister. And Chris had made Nic feel just as welcome. After the holiday break, when both Mark and Nic had returned to college in Missoula, Lauren and Chris couldn't have been happier to find out they were still dating.

Then Lauren and Chris got engaged.

Nic went into the suite, plopped down on the couch, and leaned her head back. The pressure got worse each day that fall. Lauren's hints about how perfect a double wedding would be. Chris teasingly calling her the next Vang woman. Then Christmas Eve came. They had planned to spend it together with the rest of the Vang family at a posh mountain ski town, but instead of driving her to the ski lodge, Mark drove away.

She was standing in the middle of her one-room apartment when he told her, coat on, guitar in one hand, suitcase in another. He asked her to sit down.

She remembered that Mark looked awful, but he also looked determined. Now she realized he must have been anxious to start his new life without her.

She couldn't remember what he said that morning, but she could remember how each word felt like twisting, shattering blows to her heart. Mark had practiced Christmas carols with her the night before. He'd asked her to sing and play with him on Christmas, and she was going to try. Why? Why smile and sing and encourage her, telling her she'd do great, just hours before he left? To this day, she wondered if he was that good a liar or if he had ended their relationship on a whim.

Either way, she was someone he could leave quickly. And completely. She wished she could have done the same, but she never quite shook the feeling that Mark had been wrong. That he'd walked out on something beautiful.

"Half an education can be more dangerous than none —besides being a waste of money," Chris had said. The remark could have been pointed at Mark for leaving his PT degree, or at her for abandoning her fine arts degree. Probably it was meant as a barb toward her. She'd left college a year ago, after only two semesters. She hadn't wanted to enroll in the first place, but Lauren had pushed and Mark was already enrolled.

But she couldn't blame anything on Mark. She'd had trouble long before he came along. Just thinking of it made her hands sweat and her throat close up. She stood and shook out her hands. Spending time with Mark wasn't good for her, and once again she decided this weekend couldn't be over soon enough. Just then someone knocked on the door.

Before she could reach it, the door clicked and Mark entered. He was carrying a small box, which he put in the minifridge. "I think the stress is getting to Chris and Lauren," he said.

"Stress?"

"Yeah. Lauren got talked into organizing this whole shindig—lodging, transportation, everything. And from what I can gather, the whole thing is costing them a lot of money."

"They shouldn't have to pay for anything out of pocket."

"You would think so, and that's true for a lot of stuff, but maybe they aren't getting reimbursed for everything. And neither of them is going to want to ask Mom and Dad for money." Mark leaned back against the counter and shook his head. "If I didn't know better, I'd say they're in some financial trouble."

"Lauren would tell me if she was in trouble."

"Just like you tell her when you're in trouble?"

Nic frowned. "It's not the same thing." It *was* the same thing. But she liked to think that she was less judgmental than her sister, so there was no reason for Lauren to keep secrets from her. Maybe she was wrong.

"I know what we need. We need to head down into town for the Christmas fair. Most everyone is going."

"I'm not everyone."

"No, Nic, you certainly aren't." He took her hand and pulled her toward the door. "Don't you have any last-minute shopping to do?"

She hadn't done any Christmas shopping, except for Petra and Elliot's presents. It was foolish to leave their packages where she had, and she hoped it wouldn't get the kids into trouble. "I suppose I should get something for Lauren and Chris."

"Absolutely. Even the cranky couple deserves a gift. But I should warn you, it's about ten degrees out there right now."

Nic added some long underwear under her pants and a thermal top under her sweater, plus a beautiful sage-green neck shawl a friend had knit for her. Out of habit, she checked the mirror. Her pretty wool jacket, the slim pants, and her boots all fit together. It was a good outfit for a craft fair outing.

An outing with Mark. That made her think of Tracie, Melly's cute mom. Purse in hand, she hesitantly stepped out of her room. Mark fiddled with the troublesome zipper on his parka. Seeing the coat made her heart skip, but there was no sign that he knew she'd been in his room. "You don't need to go with me," she told him. "If you have other plans."

"I have no plans," he said. "At least for tonight." He gave her a devious grin.

She didn't ask him what he meant since it was none of her business, but she assumed it had something to do with Tracie. She walked with him down the stairs, past Mr. And Mrs. Vang's conversing in the lobby, and out the front doors. The cold air made her gasp.

One of the big pine trees out front was strung all the way to the top with large white Christmas lights. Lights glittered from the front porch railings and around the big front windows, setting off a warm golden glow within. They stepped out onto the sidewalk that wound around the pond on the northwest side of the building. The pond had been groomed for ice-skating.

Old-fashioned lamps lined the walkway through a small grove of pines and down to the underpass below the highway. As they got closer, she could hear the sound of kids in the tunnel calling out "Echo!" and listening to their voices reverberate. They strolled through the well-lit tunnel soon after, commenting on the beautiful lanterns that looked like antique gaslights, and then through another tiny but dense grove of pines.

Where the path crossed a road, they had to stop for a horse-drawn wagon. It was a modest wagon with straw bales for seats, but the horses were wearing bells and the wagon had lights strung along its side. The man and woman on the driver's bench waved to Nic and Mark and the people who had come up behind them, and so did the family in the wagon.

Ahead of them was the Alhambra town square. A dormant fountain sat in the middle, and all around it were tables filled with baked goods, arts, and crafts. “Oh, look at the scarves,” Nic said as they approached.

“I’ll get us some cider and catch up,” Mark said, and she started browsing. There were only about twenty vendors in the square, but there was a wide variety of goods. By the time Mark returned, she’d purchased a set of hand-painted cards. “For Lauren?” he asked.

“Yes. She’s always been better than me at keeping in touch,” Nic said. “But I don’t know what to get Chris.”

“I saw something.” He handed her a Styrofoam cup full of hot apple cider garnished with a cinnamon stick and led her to another table. “How about this?” A girl was selling balls made out of sand and a secret ingredient, then wrapped in layers of party balloons. “Stress relievers.” He tossed one up in the air and squeezed it in his hand. “You squeeze them when you get stressed out.”

“They last a long time, guaranteed,” the young entrepreneur said.

“Chris might not think that’s funny,” Nic said.

“I do. And it’s useful. How much, young lady?” Mark asked. He handed over the two dollar bills she required, then he turned to Nic and said, “It could be from both of us.”

“That would be doubly inappropriate,” she said, wandering over to the next table. It featured clay Christmas ornaments. As soon as she spotted the sweet Jesus, Mary, and Joseph ornament, she bought it. As she paid for the ornament, she caught sight of the horse-drawn wagon across the way, making its slow circuit around the square.

"How's the cider?" he asked.

"Delicious. I'm sorry, Mark, what do I owe you for it?"

He shook his head. "Nothing, Nic. I didn't mean for you to pay me back."

"Well, it's not as if this is a date," she said. Her words fell flat.

A little line appeared between his eyebrows. "Can we sit down? Over there?" He pointed at an empty bench.

Great, just great, she thought. They had been doing just fine acting as if they'd never dated and he'd never broken her heart. Then she had to say that.

She sat down first, all the way over to one end, but he sat down in the middle, too close for her comfort. She sipped the cider while he appeared to be thinking, staring off at the lights of the craft tables. "I just wanted to say I'm sorry. You've been great. You were great back at Chris and Lauren's wedding too. And happy."

A shadow crossed his expression, and then it was gone. "And you're great now. And I was a complete jerk. And I've been a jerk every day since then because I haven't talked to you about it."

"I don't think about it very often," she said. It was another lie. But she spent less time thinking about him than she used to, she reasoned. She noticed he had the nerve to look wounded by her words.

"That's fair," he said. "But I'm grateful you're here with me now. I'm grateful that we have the chance to talk. I want to get caught up on what's going on in your life. And I don't blame you at all if you want to tell me just to shut up."

Then shut up, she thought. She hated this so much her skin crawled. The way he was sitting close beside her, leaning into her, searching her face with his gaze. It was just like the serious conversations they'd had about what they both wanted out of their lives, back when it seemed as if they were mapping out a life together. And it was also exactly like the morning he'd broken up with her. She could deal with funny and charming Mark, but this Mark —he wasn't worth the risk. Shut up, she thought again. And she had almost worked up the courage to say it out loud when his gaze flickered up, back to her, then up again. He sighed and smiled. "Hey," he called out weakly.

"I'm sorry, are we interrupting something?"

Nic heard footsteps crunching through the snow and turned to see Tracie and Melly approaching. "Not at all," Nic said. As far as she was concerned, the woman's timing was perfect.

"We were headed over there," Tracie said, pointing in another direction, "but then we saw you. We wanted to ask—"

"There's a hay ride," Melly said.

"Oh," Mark said.

"We were going to catch the wagon the next time around," Tracie said, looking sheepish.

"Sounds great," Nic said. She would find an opportunity to escape back to the hotel, and then the others could spend some time together.

Tracie smiled at her, looking grateful. Her strawberry-blond hair glowed against her silvery down jacket, and she looked both cute and comfy in sheepskin boots. Her trendy metro outfit made Nic feel dumpy, but she pushed the feelings away. It didn't matter. One day down, two to go. Then she'd figure the rest out later. Or maybe she could make her mind up tonight. She could throw a dart at a map of Montana, apply for a job, and pray no one asked for references.

"There it is! There it is!" Melly jumped up and down. "Let's get on now, Momma."

Nic placed the sound of bells and looked over her left shoulder to see the wagon approaching on the road behind them.

"No, honey, we have to go over that way," Tracie said, pointing toward the south. "That's where the ride starts."

"Oh no," Melly said.

"No problem, we can beat it," Mark said, taking the girl's hand. He waited politely for Nic to stand up and join them, and then they took off for a brisk walk. They needn't have hurried; they arrived well before the horses. Two teenagers were the only other people in line, and as they waited, Mark assured Melly that they hadn't missed the hay ride.

Standing next to Mark, Tracie, and Melly, who looked like a lovely family, Nic couldn't have felt more out of place. Mark pointed to the sign that read "$5 Suggested Donation, Alhambra Family Foundation" and informed them the ride was on him. Nic was desperate to get away, but Tracie kept drawing her into the conversation, and even Melly seemed happy to see her. She was about to make an excuse to leave when Mark waved toward the craft tables and called out, "Hey! Join us!"

Lauren and Chris. Nic believed that hayrides were romantic, and the last thing she wanted to do was ride one with her ex-boyfriend and his new flame, her sister and her husband, and the teenaged lovebirds. But Lauren was just steps away. She couldn't make a break for it now without being rude. At the very least, it would make her look suspicious.

The wagon pulled up and the driver jumped off, coming around the back to move two hay bales over to the end of the wagon to serve as a step stool for the family getting off. "Honey, you can pet him if you'd like," a woman's voice said. The older woman on the wagon seat smiled down at Melly. Melly was staring at the horse nearest to her with wide-eyed wonder.

"Oh, thank you, but..." Tracie turned and stared at Nic, who was standing right beside her. She looked stricken. "Horses," she mouthed and then grimaced. Was she scared of horses?

"Want me to?" Nic whispered, and Tracie nodded quickly.

Nic leaned down to Melly's height. "Want to pet the horse?" she asked. Melly nodded. She took the girl's tiny gloved hand in her own and walked up beside the horse's head. "What's his name?" she asked the woman in the wagon.

"Streaker," she chuckled. "Don't worry, he's not as fast as he used to be." Melly reached up to touch his shoulder, then she walked closer to the horse's head. The horse leaned down a little, blowing steamy breath out of his nostrils as he did, and Melly jumped back.

Nic held tight to her hand. "He's saying hi," she said. "Dogs sniff, horses blow. Here, watch." She leaned a little closer to the horse and blew air. Curious, the horse obliged her by turning her way and snorting a little more.

Melly giggled. "You're talking."

"Do you mind if I pick you up?" Nic asked. Melly reached her hands into the air. Seated on Nic's hip, almost at eye level, the horse must not have seemed as frightening. She pulled off one glove and reached out and touched his cheek, and Streaker blinked.

"He winked," Melly said, and Nic smiled.

"Here, touch his nose, it's as soft as velvet." She traced her fingers down the pink snip on the horse's nose, and Melly did the same.

"Soft," she said reverently.

Nic was suddenly aware that people might be waiting for her. "Ready for a ride with Streaker?" she asked, and when the little girl nodded, her curls danced over her shoulders.

Nic strode back to the wagon and lifted Melly into it, and Melly ran gleefully to her mother, saying, "Streaker is soft!"

Chris and Lauren had climbed on the wagon. Two more reasons not to ride along. But just then Melly plopped down next to her mom and patted the straw bale beside her. "Sit by me, Nickie!"

There was no way to turn down an offer like that. Besides, Mark would have paid for her ride by now. She climbed on and sat alongside Melly, who was telling her mom about Streaker. And Lauren, who had no idea that Streaker was the name of the horse, was looking concerned.

With the teenage couple riding along, the wagon was fairly full, and the driver pulled the hay bales away. It took several "Tsk" sounds and a snap of the reins to get the horses to move. "Sleepy horses," Melly observed. "Mommy, is this a one horse soap and sleigh?"

Mark took that one, singing the song very slowly to

separate the words, while Tracie looked over her daughter's head at Nic and said, "Thank you so much."

"It was fun," Nic said. "I take it you're not a big fan of—"

Tracie shook her head and put a finger to her lips, preventing Nic from saying more. "Nope. But I'm not going to let my silliness influence my brave little girl."

Nic really couldn't help but like Tracie. It would have been easier not to like her, since she was probably dating Mark, but now that wasn't an option.

"It's good to see you again," Lauren said to Tracie. "I heard you moved to Glendive."

"We did. Mark found us a place just down the road from the hotel where I'm working."

"Oh, I didn't know you found a job already," Lauren said. Her expression was cheerful, but Nic recognized an interrogation when she saw one.

"Mark got me the job too. He introduced me to the hotel manager, and they started me part time. I work the third shift while Melly's asleep."

"That's great," Lauren said with a smile. "Does your daughter go to work with you?"

There was a tiny flinch of a frown, then Tracie glanced at Mark. "No," she said hesitantly.

"Oh, that's good. So you found someone you can trust to watch her."

"Yes." More hesitation.

"Melly stays with me at the church three nights a week," Mark said. "Melly and I get up early and have breakfast together, right?"

Chris frowned, and so did Lauren, at least for a second. Nic tried not to look as surprised as they did, but she was. So Mark and Tracie did a lot more than just swim together.

"Oatmeal," Melly smiled. "And drums."

"I'm teaching her drums," Mark said, giving Tracie an awkward grin.

"That explains a few things," Tracie said with a laugh, but she and Mark were the only ones laughing, and the sound of their laughter died out quickly.

"Melly staying with him is just a temporary thing," Tracie said, turning back to face Lauren. Nic saw it again, the tired expression that made this young woman look older. "I'm looking for a roommate, someone who is around at night and doesn't mind keeping an eye on things. It's harder than it should be to find someone like that, even for cheap rent."

"We'll find someone," Mark said, giving her an encouraging look and gently touching her shoulder. Nic's heart ached. Mark and Tracie were closer than she'd imagined.

And she was happy for Tracie and happier still for Melly. No one deserved to be without a father.

Melly had started singing "Jingle Bells" by herself, although she was completely confused about the words now that they weren't what she expected. When she'd almost given up, Mark joined her song at full voice, and his voice was something to hear. So much strength, Nic marveled. When the chorus came along, Melly tugged at her mother's arm until Tracie quietly joined in. Then Melly tugged Nic's sleeve, looked up at her with big blue eyes, and said, "Sing, Nickie?"

So she did. When the chorus was over, only her and Mark sang the lesser-known verse, her personal favorite. It always made her smile. And in the cold night air their voices rang out, silly but beautiful, a resonance between them that always came so easily. They used to sing together a lot. The chorus came, and every single person on the wagon joined in, much to Melly's delight. When the song was over, they applauded each other. "Again! Again!" Melly laughed, and Tracie gave her a hug. "Soon, honey. Look, see all the lights on the houses? What do you see over there?"

"Mark, look, it's Rudolph!" Melly said, pointing to a lighted inflatable on the front lawn of a small home.

"Your voice is just as beautiful as Mark said it was," Tracie said softly. "Did you see everyone in the square looking? You and Mark sounded amazing together. I wish I could sing like that."

"Thank you, that's nice of you to say," Nic said, but before the words were out of her mouth, she felt the cold dread race up her body. She glanced toward the center of the town square. Were people staring? They were, at least a few. How many people had been listening?

Mark started singing the intro to "Rudolph the Red-Nosed Reindeer," and beside her, Melly tugged again. "Sing."

"I'm sorry," she said to the curly-haired girl, "I can't right now." Already her throat had constricted so that her voice was shaky and strained. She could feel a cold sweat breaking out on her face and the dangerous speed of her heart. Tracie gave her a questioning look, and Nic tried to smile and shrug, but she could feel her lips quivering. She looked away, but there was no place to hide. She found herself facing Lauren, who looked stricken. She knew.

Nic tried to find a neutral place to look, so she turned her gaze toward Mark without meeting his eye. Instead, she stared at the neon-colored zipper on his parka. Humiliation washed over her as it always did, following the anxiety like an evil twin. She did her deep-breathing exercises. She worked to distract her mind and to convince her body that she wasn't about to die. She did almost everything all the professors and counselors had said to do, and it was enough to keep her from passing out, but she couldn't sing. She'd be lucky if she was able to sleep tonight, she thought.

The song was short. Nic plastered a smile on her face and clapped loudly at the end, whistling as she did.

At least she could still whistle. She looked the other way, back over her shoulder, focusing on the beautiful Christmas lights. There was something, from a lighted star to a whole nativity to choreographed marquee lights, on every house that faced the town square. And as far as she could tell, most of the other houses in the tiny town as well. She could feel the chill as her body started to calm down. When she glanced at Tracie, she found a sympathetic expression.

Did she know about her stage fright? Mark had mentioned her to Tracie, so maybe she did. But there was something in that look that said Tracie understood, and that it was okay.

Nic felt a twinge of regret that she wouldn't have a chance to get to know her better. After Christmas, Tracie would be going back to Glendive. With Mark. And Nic would be going anywhere but Glendive. Or Missoula.

The wagon made another turn, the homestretch into the parking lot, and slowly pulled to a stop. The moment she stepped down from the wagon and off a hay bale,

Lauren grabbed her arm and started walking. "Talk to me," she said.

Partly because it would cause a scene to break free from Lauren's grip, and partly because she knew her sister was genuinely concerned, she walked. Lauren sat them both down on a nearby bench. "I thought you were doing rehabilitation."

"It's not an addiction."

Lauren huffed, and a thin stream of steam came from her lips. "You know what I mean."

"I was in counseling for a year." On and off.

"Nic, it's gotten worse. How could it get worse if you're trying to fix it? You've got to stop quitting things." Her voice cut. Lauren's worry looked so much like anger that Nic had a hard time telling where one ended and the other began.

She looked over her sister's shoulder. Where had Mark gone? Somewhere with Tracie, no doubt. Chris was there, milling around under the lamplight where they'd left him.

I didn't quit Mark, Nic thought. He quit me.

Lauren wasn't finished. "Money matters, Nicole. You took all that time off after high school to…" Lauren's hand fluttered through the air as she searched for the right word.

Work. And grieve, Nic thought.

"Grow," Lauren said, rolling her eyes as she did. "As if odd jobs will help you grow. Then you went to school for one year—one year! And then you quit. Again. How long is this going to go on?"

"I'm done with school, Lauren." It was the first time she'd said it out loud. With it came a feeling of certainty.

Lauren blinked several times. "I don't believe that. I

know things have been hard for you. First Mom passing, then this anxiety disorder, then Mark." Her lips narrowed to a thin line. "You've got to fight through this, Nic."

Nic leaned back against the cold wooden slats of the park bench. Lauren wanted what was best for her. So had Mom. She wanted it for both her girls. But Lauren had built a life, and Nic had nothing to show for the years that had passed.

Lauren was so certain that the key to everything was a college degree. That was where their portions of their mother's life insurance were supposed to go. Lauren always said it was what Mom would have wanted. If so... "Lauren, why didn't you go to college?"

"This isn't about me."

"Yes, it is. It's about you and me. You got a college fund, too. Why haven't you gone?"

Lauren looked as if she'd been slapped. "You wouldn't understand. In the real world, things don't always go the way you want."

There were a few things Nic would have liked to say to that, but she didn't. Nic had a very good understanding of how things didn't always turn out as expected. But Mom had a saying for times like this: sometimes the words that bless the most are the ones you choose not to say.

She missed her mom, and she missed the time when Lauren didn't feel like she had to be a second mother. Back when Lauren was her sister.

"I don't miss school," Nic said. "I don't miss performing."

"Well, that's because of your anxiety disorder."

"Lauren, I said I don't miss performing. I never liked orchestras, and I never wanted to be a singer-songwriter, the next phenom, or a music teacher. The only thing I ever liked was singing and playing guitar with friends or by myself, and I know more than enough to be able to do that."

"How can you not want a degree?"

"What for?"

"Respect. And a good paying job."

Nic looked at her sister, pleading with her eyes for Lauren to try to understand. "I'm not going back to school." At least now, and probably never for a music degree. She was happy to work as a nanny, and she'd do it again in a heartbeat. And someday, maybe, she'd be blessed with kids of her own.

"But you were brilliant," Lauren said, a note of disgust in her voice.

That startled Nic. Was Lauren jealous? It was no great talent she was wasting. She was skilled, she was diligent, and she had a good voice. Lauren was the one with straight As all through school. "You should go back to school, Lauren. You were always better at it than me."

"The money's gone."

What? Nic's mind whirled with possibilities. Lauren would never have squandered it. Had it been stolen?

"We used it to start Chris's business."

Nic tried to remember what it was Chris had been doing lately. Opening some accounting firm with a friend, doing taxes and such for online businesses. She remembered that Chris often talked about retiring in twenty years, it would be so profitable. "You'll get it back soon."

"That was the plan," Lauren said. She smirked. "We thought we just had to get to tax season, and we'd be in the money. Now he's not even sure he can keep the doors open until February. He's started looking for another job." She frowned at Nic. "Now we can't help you if you get in trouble."

Nic blinked. She had never once asked Lauren for money, but still Lauren looked pained, as if by not having something set aside to aid her helpless little sister, she was a failure. Nic had never been without a job for long. It was the good jobs that had been few and far between. Nic tried not to feel offended. Lauren was worried about her.

Nic couldn't think of something to say that wouldn't aggravate or insult her sister, so she just put her arm around Lauren's shoulders. "Chris is looking anxious. You shouldn't keep him waiting so long."

"It's good for him." Lauren crossed her arms and pouted.

It was so unlike Lauren that Nic giggled. "You love him. And you love me. Come on." They walked back just as the wagon was pulling into the parking area again. Before she could get drawn in, Nic waved good-bye, tucked her hands deep in her pockets, and headed to the hotel at a brisk pace.

In the empty hotel suite, she cleaned up, put on flannel pajamas, and put her tablet on the bed. Propping herself up on her elbows, she connected to the hotel's Internet service. She wanted to look for job opportunities online. The only problem was… where? She was ready to leave Missoula. She hoped to stay in Montana, but maybe a little time away would do her good. But evidently "west of the Mississippi" wasn't a valid search term.

Moreover, she wasn't going to find the perfect job and get hired by Christmas, although she wished she could. Then she could reassure her sister. Or was it Lauren's approval Nic was seeking? There wasn't much difference between the two. She turned the tablet off and dropped her head face first onto the soft covers.

Knock knock. "Nic?"

Go away, Nic thought. "Yes?" she called out. The down covers muffled her voice.

"I have something for you."

With a soft moan, she dragged herself to her feet and opened the door. Mark's face was hidden by the lid of a cardboard box, open to show two pieces of pie and one large wedge of cheddar cheese.

"Sold," she said.

He set it on the coffee table and sat down on the couch, baiting her to join him with the extra fork in his hand. "Only one piece of cheese? You're a coward."

"Mine is blueberry pie," he said. "What kind of idiot would mix blueberries with cheese?"

"The French. In a crepe." She took the piece of cheese and broke it into smaller pieces, which she spread neatly over the top crust of the apple pie. Mark watched her, and she saw a grin tugging at his mouth. "And if you're going to make fun of me I want my own plate," she added.

"No, no. I'm just appreciating your workmanship. You want it just so, and you make it that way."

"Well, if I don't I might run out of cheese before the pie is done, or the other way around."

His eyes lingered on her as if he was going to say something more, and then he dug into his dessert and ate a huge bite, smiling as he chewed. "I know. You're not the kind of girl a guy could forget."

Nic cut off a small slice of the apple pie with her fork, then cut it in half again and set her fork down. She was sitting so close to him, bumping shoulders. It had felt natural a moment ago, but now it felt wrong.

"So how long have you and Tracie been dating?" she asked.

Mark cut a glance at her. "What makes you think we're dating?"

"It's pretty obvious. Either you are or you want to be."

"You think it's pretty obvious, huh?" Mark grinned at her and ate another bite of blueberry pie. "Only one problem with that theory. I don't date married women."

"She's still married?"

Mark nodded. "And she'll stay that way unless Cole divorces her, and I don't see that happening."

Nic tried to process that new information. Did that mean she'd been wrong? But Mark's fondness for Tracie had been so clear. Maybe he was hoping for more but couldn't have it. She knew how that felt. "I'm sorry," she said.

"Yeah, me too. Not that I want them to divorce, I'm just sorry that he's making it so hard." He glanced at her, frowning. "Wait a second. Did you mean you feel sorry for me? You think…?" Mark leaned backward, putting his arm on the couch back and tilting his head. "Well, that explains a couple things."

Nic didn't understand where he was headed, but she could tell he was teasing her. She crossed her arms. "What explains what?"

"Like how much you've been avoiding me. You won't look me in the eye, you won't—"

"I've been perfectly polite. Are all the girls you dump as polite as me?" She tried to keep her voice playful. She wasn't sure if she'd succeeded.

The smirk left his face. “No, Nic. You’ve been amazing. But Tracie loves Cole, and I’m not interested, and above all else, eww. She’s my cousin-in-law. It’d be like dating my cousin.”

“I’m your sister-in-law and you dated me. What is that like?”

“It’s not like that. Besides, you’re my sister-in-law’s sister. That’s not like a sister, that’s like a…”

“Yes?”

“A mutual friend of people I love.”

She wrinkled her nose. “Nice try.” She took a bite of her pie, the cheese balanced on top.

“Nic, I took this babysitting job because I wanted to see you.”

Her heart pounded, but she didn’t look at him. How was she supposed to respond to that? She was sure he didn’t mean much by it. Or mean anything at all. And he'd better not mean it *that* way. And if he did, he was an insensitive jerk because she’d just spent a year getting over him and there was no way on earth she was going to get suckered in now by blue eyes and a kind word.

But what if he did mean it that way?

She looked at what remained of her pie and thought about Elliot and Petra. It was past time for their bedtime snack, and with the holiday busyness in the Gordon household, she was sure no one would think of it.

It was almost ten o’clock, or close enough. She’d made it through the day. But she just couldn’t take any more disappointment now, especially from Mark. “Time for bed, good night,” she said, and she hurried to her room and shut the door.

What on earth was he doing? Did he think it was fair

to toy with her feelings again? She shook her head. She didn't know what Mark was thinking, and it didn't matter. She was the one acting as if they were a happy couple, sharing with him, sitting beside him. And sharing a suite. She needed distance from him, and time.

But hundreds of miles and a whole year hadn't been enough to fade her feelings for him.

Nic buried herself under the blankets and pillows and lay still, thinking of Elliot and Petra, her kids. But they weren't hers at all. She had no right to a future with them. Or Mark, for that matter. And just when she decided she was strong enough to put it all behind her, she thought about the presents in the closet, under the blanket, in the house in Missoula she would never enter again. That's when the tears finally came.

CHRISTMAS EVE

"Wake up, sleepyhead."

Nic had a hard time emerging from the drowsy cocoon where she'd been sleeping. She placed Mark's voice first, and the rest followed: hotel, Christmas, babysitting. "I'm up," she lied.

"I got breakfast and a cup of coffee for you."

It occurred to her that she could hear that every single day for the rest of her life and never grow tired of it. "Thank you. I'll be right out." She pictured him coming into her room with a tray of food and a steaming mug, setting it on the fluffy bedding, and sitting down beside her. He would sing Greg Brown's song "Good Morning Coffee" to her. In her mind, he also wore that goofy orange bathing suit so she could see the taut muscles of his arms and chest.

That thought woke her up enough that she came to her senses. She'd figured it all out last night. No matter what Mark felt for her, he had left her. He had made that decision, and for an entire year he had happily lived without her. Sure, she still had feelings for Mark, and maybe she even still loved him, but she wasn't going to go down that road again. And if he thought he could toy with her feelings, he had another thing coming.

Dreamy little fantasies about him weren't going to help at all.

Nic got up and pulled her hair back in a ponytail. She washed her face, put on sun block, quickly donned the layers she'd need, including her ski jacket, then tossed her goggles, hat, and gloves in a tote bag. She decided to wear a pair of athletic pants and pack her bulky ski pants into the tote, then change at the ski area.

Mark was ready to go as well, his gear in a pile. He handed her coffee in a paper cup without looking her in the eye. "Should be a fun morning," he said, but he didn't sound like he believed it.

Nic wondered if he hadn't been doing some thinking too.

He handed her a plate as well, and she sat down at the breakfast bar. There were eggs, a waffle, and some fruit. And the rest of her pie, which made her smile.

"I think we should take turns on the bunny hill, so we each get some real skiing in."

She convinced him that she was fine staying on the bunny hill all morning, and the truth was she enjoyed helping the littlest ones learn how to maneuver in the snow. In return, he insisted that he should drive. She hurried to finish her breakfast and trotted down the stairs. If she was fast enough, she could have her skis and boots out and away from her car before he even knew where she was parked.

The sun was up, but it hadn't reached into the mountain valley yet. The sky above was the deep blue of a high-altitude winter, and the air was sharp, but the sunlight would soon change that. She spotted him across the parking lot, and she hunched her shoulders and tucked her hands deep in her pockets. He waved her over to a small silver SUV. "Welcome to my mom car," he said.

"You got rid of your Dodge."

"Technically, it got rid of me. When Ingrid got a new car, I offered to buy it because I know how crazy Edward is about maintaining their cars. They only charged me the trade-in value. All-wheel drive CR-V and merely 100,000 miles." He opened the passenger door for her, then hustled a couple microwaveable curry soup bowls from the floor to the rear of the car.

She wouldn't have called it a mom car, but it did have a family-friendly vibe about it. "Congratulations, it's nice."

"Edward had it detailed twice a year. Poor car, it'll never have it that good again." He closed the door for her and walked around to the other side.

Something about the car made her feel awkward. It was as if it meant something more about him, something sensible and grown-up.

Or maybe it didn't, and it didn't matter either way.

He fit the skis inside between the seats, and they started out. It was about a forty-minute drive to the ski area, and along the way Nic learned that Mark had become the youth leader at his church. When he'd bragged about the kids from the youth group the day before, he'd neglected to say that he was the adult in charge.

The church was too small to afford a youth pastor position, and that was why they'd given him the custodian duties and let him live on site. It wasn't all fun and games. The population of the town was in flux, and churches were the target of those who wanted to ask for money as well as those who would rather steal it. He had a couple harrowing stories to tell, but it didn't seem to bother him.

"I bet it seems weird to you," he said, "that my favorite job is one I don't even get paid for."

"No, it doesn't." Nic could see how much he loved it. She'd never seen him so excited about work before. This sort of enthusiasm had always been reserved for outdoor hobbies and music, or perhaps hitting the driving range.

He had been enthusiastic about her once. Or maybe she'd imagined it.

"But I don't get paid," he repeated. His blue eyes were dark, and he glanced at her as if he was waiting for her approval.

"That's not true. They pay you what they can." She wondered what Chris would think about the whole thing, and she realized he probably would view it the same way Lauren looked at Nic's job—that it wasn't a real job. "I understand. Being a nanny was the best job I ever had. I know people think I'm insane for not going back to school."

"Was." He glanced her way again. "You said your nanny job *was* the best job."

Ahead of them the road was climbing higher. Packed snow covered it completely, and to either side was a small wall of snow made by the snowplows. "Please don't mention it to Lauren and Chris yet."

"I knew you didn't work there anymore. Something about the way you talked at lunch with Mom and Dad.

Since talking about it made you sad, I guessed you got laid off."

"I quit." She watched the road climb into the sunshine. "But I had to."

Mark was quiet for a moment, but she could tell he was waiting. "Do you want to talk about it?"

"Not now. Not really."

He nodded. "Okay. But I'm going to ask again."

"I'm sure you will," she said, giving him a wry smile. She knew he meant it, and it felt good to know he cared. Mark didn't just listen, he remembered. And she'd missed that.

A valley opened up ahead of them, and they pulled into a parking lot that was already more than half full of cars. Evidently the Vang family wasn't the only one that thought Christmas Eve was an excellent time to go skiing.

Despite having a rendezvous site, it was chaotic gathering all the kids and their equipment and getting rentals. They straightened out which kids had what experience, and more important, who could be expected to ride on a lift without incident. Soon she was on the fenced-off bunny hill with Sebastian, Melly, and Eddie, and Mark was riding the ski lift with the other kids.

The sun was brilliant above and below on the snow, and the kids were more than warm enough in their snowsuits. The bunny hill had a "magic carpet ride" instead of a ski lift, a moving sidewalk in the snow that fascinated the kids. Sebastian took to the hill like a determined soldier, doing everything she said and never wavering. Soon he'd made friends with another boy about the same age and at the same skill level.

But Nic had a hard time convincing Eddie—once he

got past her—to make a few turns rather than ski straight down at the highest possible speed. It was no small task tugging him back up the hill.

Nic's second job was to get Melly to go faster. It wasn't the girl's first time on skis, and she seemed to do well. She was old enough to go on the bigger slope, but she had no interest in leaving the sunny confines of the magic carpet slope. Nic raced her and did a spectacular pratfall to show her that falling was survivable, and she managed to get her to go a little faster. She felt that Melly was on the edge of breaking through, but they were running out of time.

Lunchtime was the end of the day for the kids. Everyone but Tegan had rented equipment, and so as parents escorted the others to return their things, Tegan talked Mark into one more trip.

Tracie was there as well, in her snow boots and jeans. "Aren't you going to ski?" Mark asked.

She shook her head. "We didn't do a lot of that in Nevada," she said. "I'd like to learn."

"I'd be happy to..." Nic began, and then her brain kicked into gear. What was she saying? Tracie lived as far away as Mark. And Nic lived nowhere at all. How could she offer to give her lessons? But both Tracie and Mark were staring at her. "To take Melly up on the lift just once," she said. "If you don't mind waiting."

"That would be great," Tracie said. "If the other kids get back before you, I'll round them up."

Melly looked up at Nic with wide eyes.

"Would you please hold my hand for the ride up?" Nic asked the girl.

It took a few words of encouragement from Tracie, but Melly surprised her by saying, "I'll hold your hand."

Mark and Nic skied down and across the slope to the chair lift. The hardest part was the short wait, and she could see the wheels turning in Melly's helmeted head. But the operator slowed the lift down so much that it was no problem getting Melly where she needed to be in time. The chair swept them up and away, and Nic hooked up her poles as a safety belt, but she hardly needed to. She had a good hold on the chair and Melly, who was clinging fast to the chair.

Nic pointed out the beautiful, snow-covered trees, and the one tree adorned with strings of beads thrown from the chair lift. She wondered out loud if many people had done that, or maybe it had been one enterprising lift rider, throwing necklaces over and over again. For some reason, the thought of that made Melly giggle.

In the chair ahead of them, Mark had a death grip on Tegan, who was jumping around with no heed to how far above the ground they were. "I think Tegan ate jumping beans," Nic said. Then she had to explain what those were, although Melly didn't believe one word of her explanation.

They rehearsed the dismount, and when they arrived, things went well. Nic took hold of Melly's hood and held her upright, and gravity did the rest.

The slope at the top was the worst, and Nic wondered why that was so often the case. She stopped beside Mark, who was giving an impatient Tegan a lecture about being under control. Nic got the feeling it wasn't the first time he'd done that.

She gave Melly a different pep talk, and then because she wasn't sure Melly would go at all if Nic went on ahead, she sent her off on her own and followed close behind her. Melly went down the steepest part, got her bearings, and turned until she not only stopped but also faced up the hill. Nic praised her, but the smile on the girl's face said it all.

The rest of the trip was all fun. "It's just like sledding!" Melly kept saying. Nic spoke nothing but compliments. Teaching time was over; it was time to celebrate the girl's newfound skills.

They even passed Mark and Tegan, who, it appeared, were having another discussion. Mark's body posture was much more adamant than the last time, and Nic wondered what had happened.

The bunny hill joined with an intermediate slope in a wide chute near the bottom, and it was there that Tegan flew past them. At the same time, she heard Mark calling out behind her, "Slow down!"

But there was something in Tegan's stiff, awkward posture that made her think he wasn't able to. Nic stopped Melly, thinking she might need to ski on alone to help, but Mark passed her at that instant, tucked low and calling, "Look out!" She wasn't sure if he was calling to Tegan or the other skiers on the slope.

There was no way she could catch up. "Oh no," Melly said, and Nic watched as the young boy raced across the busy slope. One skier barely stopped in time to avoid a collision. And Tegan kept going straight up the slope on the other side. There was no way he could avoid hitting the trees.

Mark was there in an instant. It happened so fast she wasn't certain how he did it. One second he was behind Tegan, tossing his poles away, and then Tegan was in his arms. He turned at the top part of the slope as if it was a half-pipe, leaving a huge rooster tail of snow. For a heart-stopping moment, they were perpendicular to the ground. Then Mark jumped and got his skis beneath him, dropped down, and miraculously came to a stop. Nic realized she was shaking.

"Let's get Uncle Mark's sticks, okay, Nic?" Melly said.

Nic nodded. She was pretty sure the little girl had no idea how close her cousin had just come to a serious injury.

They skied slowly across the slope, Nic backtracking a little to get the poles, and then they went down the short and gentle slope that remained. When she got there, she saw Mark talking to his brother Jim, Tegan's father. Evidently he'd seen some of what had happened because he was speaking sharply to Tegan.

Tegan looked scared to death. Whether that was because of his father or his runaway ride, Nic had no idea.

She and Melly steered their way over to Tracie, who was as proud of her daughter as Melly was. Tracie took off her daughter's skis. "Thank you so much, Nic," she said. "You're amazing."

"It was all Melly."

"Did you see that?" Tracie said, tipping her head toward Tegan as she helped Melly put on her snow boots.

"Yes. I almost had a heart attack."

"Mark has some pretty mad skills," Tracie said. And with a grin she added, "Admit it. You gotta love a man who can shred."

Nic didn't know how to respond. Did Tracie have feelings for Mark?

Tracie stood. "Not to mention that he just rescued a

small child." She elbowed Nic. "Aw, come on. You've got to at least think he's cute. You did go out with him."

Nic suddenly got the feeling that Tracie was playing matchmaker. It didn't make any sense. "Cute, yes. Love him for his shredding, no."

Tracie's expression fell. She looked away and said softly, "That's too bad. Hey, I'll take care of Melly's stuff. Looks like they're all meeting over there." She said good-bye to Melly and promised to see them at the hotel in a couple hours, reminding Melly that she would get to go swimming again in the meantime.

Nic took off her skis. She felt as if she'd said something wrong. She really should have been more complimentary to Mark. He deserved it, and he and Tracie were friends. Or maybe she'd misread the whole conversation. It wouldn't have been the first time.

Mark was surrounded by kids, including Tegan, who looked none the worse for wear. She studied the boy's face, and the only thing she noticed different about him was the way he kept looking at Mark as if he hung the moon. Maybe Tracie had a point; good skiing could be love-worthy.

"Are you okay?" she asked, tugging at Mark's sleeve.

He looked at her with a haggard face and wide eyes. "I don't know which is worse, losing him or facing his dad. But Jim's okay with it. Tegan's escaped from him too. We just stopped for a second to help a girl who had fallen, and the next thing I knew..."

The image of Tegan racing toward the trees struck her again, and just the thought of it made her heart race. Nic lifted up onto the toes of her ski boots and wrapped her arms around Mark's neck. "You were amazing," she said softly.

He put his hands around her waist and laughed. "I was lucky. No, make that blessed. I'm not the one who got him through the crowd without incident."

He didn't let go. She leaned back, feeling suddenly self-conscious, and Mark smiled at her, his face as bright as the sunlit snow. It took her breath away. I've missed you, she thought.

"Well hello," her sister said from behind her, and Nic jumped. She backed away in time to see Lauren and Chris walking toward them. "We're here to help you transport the kids back to the hotel." She gave Nic a pointed glance. "And just in time," she added with a smile.

Chris rode in Mark's SUV along with Tegan and his brothers, which left Nic with Lauren and all the others in her new car, a pearl-white Escalade. She had an assortment of car seats inside, and the kids seemed to know which seat belonged to each kid. "This is nice, Lauren," Nic said. "I didn't know you got a new car."

"I didn't, the company did," Lauren said curtly.

It was immaculate inside. Once everyone had settled in, Nic got in the passenger seat and smiled as Lauren started driving down the long ski-area road. "It won't look this good after you have kids," she teased.

Lauren stiffened.

Now what had she said? "It looks really good now, though," she added.

"A lot less crowded than yours, but that's not hard to do," Lauren replied. "Why did you say your car was so full?"

Lauren's memory was sufficient to remember that

herself. "Because I'm donating some stuff." She'd asked Mark not to say anything to Chris and Lauren, but that wasn't fair. She took a glance back at the carful of kids, who were distracted by each other and a cartoon playing on the in-car movie system. "And because I moved out of the Gordon house."

"Why?"

Nic didn't feel strong enough to talk about it, and she sure wasn't going to explain herself in front of the kids. "I needed to quit."

Lauren glowered, then she made a confused little puffing sound, then she shook her head. "Now what, Nic?" Her voice had a high-pitched edge to it, but the kids behind them just kept telling ski stories to each other.

"Now I get a new job."

"What if you don't? Tim Gordon is a very influential man. I can't imagine he's happy with you leaving."

Nic didn't say anything to that, but a storm started inside her that made her throat tighten. Her breathing came fast and shallow. She'd rather think of anything other than *him*.

"What if you can't get a job in Missoula?" Lauren went on. "No one is going to hire you. Your work history is so spotty. A waitress, sales person, cashier. This was your first real job."

Nic didn't remind her that Lauren had never considered nanny a real job before. "Can we talk about this later?" Nic said softly.

Lauren was quiet for less than a minute, but at least she kept her voice down when she started in again. "How could you do this to me? I told you money is tight. For all I know we won't even have a house in a few months. How am I supposed to pay for housing for you too?"

"You don't," Nic said firmly, hoping her sister would drop it.

"Oh, right," she said, her voice rising again. "I'm supposed to leave my sister homeless. You are, aren't you? You're literally homeless, and Dad's off in Georgia with Tamara. What am I supposed to do?"

Nic noticed the kids growing quiet in the background. "Lauren—"

"And now you're fooling around with Mark as if he didn't mess your life up enough before!" Lauren wasn't even trying to be quiet now. "What are you going to do, marry him? He's a custodian living off the mercy of a tiny church in a tiny town—do you think he can support you? And then you'll get pregnant, and I'll get stuck trying to support you all. You, Mark, and Chris, his stupid accounting business, this stupid car payment, my dream house that we're going to have to sell, but it doesn't matter that this house has the perfect nursery because you'll be the only one having kids. Because Chris and I can't afford them!"

The Escalade was deathly quiet.

Nic noticed Lauren looking up in the rearview mirror, and the expressions on the little faces she saw there must have been enough to make tears spring to her eyes. She scrunched her face up. Nic knew anger was easier for Lauren to bear than embarrassment.

The talking slowly regenerated behind them, and Nic didn't say a word. At one point, she reached out to put a hand on her sister's shoulder, but Lauren shrugged it off. They arrived at the hotel, and Lauren pulled up beside

Mark's car. After she helped Nic get everything and everyone out of the car, Chris got in the passenger seat and the two drove off.

Mark and Nic were left standing in the middle of a pile of sports gear and hungry kids. "Nice trip?" he asked.

"Aunt Lauren is mad," Ella provided helpfully. "Because Nic's gonna have a baby."

Somewhere in the middle of the chaos and the craziness Lauren had thought to order pizza, and it was warm and ready when they finally got all the kids piled into the room. As soon as everyone was eating, Nic pulled Mark over to the breakfast bar to share the bare bones of Lauren's monologue. She told him just enough to put the baby comment in context.

"And I guess you were right about stress and money problems," she admitted.

"It would have been better if I'd been wrong," he answered.

"And thanks for backing me up with the kids when I said I wasn't pregnant."

He chuckled. "Hopefully by the time we swim them into oblivion they'll forget all about it." Then, more seriously, "I'm sorry."

"I'm sorry for Lauren. She always takes on so much. And she accomplishes so much."

"But if she didn't?"

"She thinks the world will come to an end," Nic sighed.

"It won't. It'll just fall apart. Like your job, Chris's business, and your mystery reason for quitting. And in time everything will get sorted out. Sometimes it even gets better, you know. God has a pretty good handle on things no matter what our intentions are."

"Yeah," she answered, but she wanted to say, "I hope so." Her mind wandered down a trail of Lauren's worries and came to rest on her mother's death and how it had affected them all. "It's been hard on Lauren since Mom died."

"You, too," he said, bumping his shoulder against hers. "But it looks to me like you're doing great."

That was the first time anyone, even her friends, had said something like that to her. She dismissed it as flattery. "Right, I'm unemployed, homeless, and—"

"I wasn't talking about that. I was talking about who you are. It looks to me like you're just fine. Better than fine."

She wondered what Mark saw when he looked so deeply into her eyes. Was he right? In a strange way, she agreed with him. No matter what her life looked like from the outside, she was proud of the work she'd done for the Gordons. And she was proud of the patience she'd gained and the fun side of herself she'd discovered when she was with Petra and Elliot.

Mark was still looking at her, a faint smile playing around the corners of his mouth, looking slightly disreputable with stubble growing and his helmet-styled mess of hair. He leaned closer—or did she?—then glanced down at her lips. Good grief, was he considering kissing her? Did he think since he'd already kissed her, she'd forever be on call for his whims?

So she spun her chair around. "How is everyone doing?" she said, her voice too loud for the room.

"Good."

Nic got her plate and put a little space between her and the blue-eyed man.

Lauren had written specific orders that the kids were not to swim for thirty minutes after they finished eating, and although Nic thought the prescription was an old wives' tale, she kept track of the time. But the roomful of refueled kids practically vibrated with energy. Nic brought out her guitar and sat down on the arm of the couch. A few chords into one of Petra and Elliot's favorite silly songs, she had most everyone's attention.

Including Mark, who was grinning from ear to ear.

By the end of the song, all the kids knew the chorus and were singing along. Loudly so. So she picked another silly song. Ella screamed, "We know this!" and she danced the hand movements as they went. One more song and it was time to change for swimming, which was simple because Lauren had thought ahead to ask the parents to dress the kids in swimsuits under their ski clothes.

The kids made a loud, singing parade on the way down to the pool, and this time everyone was eager to get in. Mark led them up the covered stairway that led to the top of the twisting tunnel slide, and Nic waited at the bottom of the slide to help catch the little ones. Everyone, from tiny Sebastian to Melly, loved that.

Mark let Tegan go by himself a few times, but Nic saw him keep an eye on the boy. The rest of the crew got into an old-fashioned game of Marco Polo that involved a lot of giggling and squealing. Since Mark let himself get caught, he was the hunter most of the time. And he was fast. He even caught Nic once, but she accused him of cheating. How could he sense where she'd gone unless he'd peeked?

The second time he came for her, he pulled her under by her ankle. When she came up for air, she was surrounded by small defenders, or at least that's what they thought they were, squealing and yelling at Mark while hanging from her. She caught her breath again before he tugged her down, and this time she twisted underwater and pushed down on his shoulders with her hands in a useless effort to keep him dunked. He rose up, and Nic found herself perched on her knees on the back of his shoulders, laughing.

"Should I throw her into the air?" Mark asked the squealing kids.

The girls screamed no while the boys screamed yes, and with a heavy push off the bottom and his hands on her legs, Mark tossed Nic over backward and away from the kids. There was no way to land gracefully, so she went down awkwardly, turned like a dolphin underwater, and headed back up to the surface.

He was right there, his arms around her. "Are you all right? I didn't mean to throw you so hard."

She gave him a look of mock outrage. "I'm wounded," she said, putting the back of her hand to her forehead.

He pulled her a little closer, and beneath the surface of the bath-warm water, she felt her legs brush against his. "I'll make it better," he growled.

But the herd of kids reached him, and he obliged by going under dramatically as they fought to dunk him.

They'd been so active that it took a long time for anyone to show signs of feeling cold, but soon Nic spotted Eddie and Sebastian shivering. And Melly and Eva had taken to holding on to the edge of the pool rather than playing, she noticed. She gathered them up and showered them off in the room again, wrapping them with fresh towels she'd snagged at the pool.

It made her heart warm when they asked her to sing. This time she stuck to a couple old folk songs, and soon the foursome were leaning against each other, cuddled on the couch, eyes droopy.

When the others joined them, they were less noisy than the day before. In fact, they were shivering and whiny, and Mark had his hands full rinsing them off. They came out of the bathroom in dripping suits and pouty faces, and Nic grabbed every towel she could find and squeezed them into one damp cuddle pile with the others.

And she sang again. She knew what she was doing, choosing one of Mark's favorites, and he didn't disappoint. His smooth voice wrapped around her own, weaving beautifully with the guitar and her voice. The song filled the room and mesmerized the kids. And when they came to the chorus, Melly sang along. The beauty that her tiny voice added, singing a song more than a hundred years older than herself, was so lovely it brought tears to Nic's eyes.

Mark sat by her, balancing himself on the opposite arm of the chair. He whispered the name of a lullaby, and they sang it together. By then a few of the kids were still awake, but no one wanted to move. She handed the guitar to him.

"I hate playing after you," he said. "You make me look like the two-bit musician I am."

She shook her head. "That's silly. Just play."

He played a popular, longer version of "Amazing Grace," one with an added chorus, but he didn't leave out a single verse of the original. He was that way. They both were. To do otherwise would have been like skipping parts of a book. They took their time, and Nic became lost in the song and the music they made together. When it was over, someone knocked at the door.

It was Tracie, and Jim and Ingrid.

"We didn't want to interrupt," Tracie said with a grin. A few of the kids were carried out while others mumbled or whimpered their way out of the room. "I don't know how they're going to make it through dinner," Mark said. "It's only an hour away."

"I could take a nap, too," Nic said. "Seven kids. If little Cici had been old enough to ski, I'd probably be dead right now. Remind me someday I don't want to have seven kids." She sat down on the couch and found it uncomfortably damp, but she couldn't bear to get up again.

"Fine. I'll remind you that you only want to have six. And you can't go to sleep now. I tell you what, you get ready, and I'll take you down to the bar for a snack and a glass of wine before dinner."

"Does that mean we're dining at the high table again? Or worse, with my sister and your brother?"

He laughed. "How about with Tracie and Melly instead?"

"Yessss," she said, high-fiving the air above her. "I can do that." Then she dragged herself into the bathroom. The floor was soaked. Water was even splashed up on the mirror. The entire suite was probably soaked.

Once again she'd forgotten to bring in a change of clothes, but it didn't matter. Mark was nowhere to be seen when she slipped into her room. She chose a nice pair of corduroys, ankle boots, and her favorite, and only, cashmere-blend sweater. It had been a present from Lauren last year. And this year her sister would be getting greeting cards in return. Hand-painted and beautiful, yes, but still—Nic sighed. She was always successful at letting her sister down.

She could hear Mark taking a shower, and she remembered him sitting in his bathing suit, a towel draped over his shoulders, inches away from her and singing. It made her wince to think of it now. It felt too intimate. And so had swimming together, especially when he'd put his arms around her, arms warmer than the hot-springs water.

She plugged in her hair dryer and drowned out her thoughts.

When she came out, she found the wet towels gone and the couch draped in clean, dry towels. She figured Mark had gone down to the pool to switch them out. The radio was playing, and two glasses of wine sat on the coffee table, along with a tiny plate piled high with orange, fish-shaped crackers.

Mark peeked out of his room. He'd shaved.

"I walked by the bar on my way to drop off the towels," he said. "Chris and Lauren are in the bar with Jim. There's no way we could have gotten out of joining them." Both of Mark's brothers and Nic's sister? She agreed they probably couldn't have made a getaway.

"And the crackers?"

He looked guilty. "I stole a plate from the bar. They had crackers sitting on all the tables. I didn't want to cheat you out of the bar experience. Take whichever glass you'd like best," he said, disappearing into his room.

She sat down on the dry towels, which were a couple layers thick, and chose the glass of white wine. Mark emerged wearing a nice shirt and a tweed jacket over dark jeans. He looked unbelievably handsome in a quirky professor sort of way. He sat down beside her, took his glass in his hand, leaned back, and said, "Tell me why you quit your job."

"This was all a ploy to get me to talk," she said. And a good one, she thought.

"Some of it was a ploy. The rest of it was me being nice. Now spill it."

Nic took a deep breath. I can do this, she thought. Please, Jesus, don't let me cry in front of Mark. "The day I left, Tim—" It felt uncomfortable calling him that. It always had, but he'd insisted. "Tim Gordon called me into his office. He started saying nice things about everything I do for the kids. And for him. I thought he was going to give me a raise. It was stupid. His office is off-limits to me and the kids. I should have known."

"He made a pass at you?"

"Yes." She remembered to breathe. "I thought he was going to give me a raise. Can you imagine? I was so blind."

"You couldn't stay there after that." It was a statement.

"No," she agreed. "I told him I was going to start looking for another job, and it made him angry. He said I was betraying the kids. He said I'd led him on." The tears were threatening already. There was more—his anger, the necklace, and other things she didn't want to relive. "I don't know what I did wrong. He's a deacon at our church. He's so well-known, and everybody says the nicest things about him and his wife."

"Did you have feelings for him?" Mark asked. There was nothing accusing in his voice, but she cringed.

"No. He just intimidated me. And the kids. But I did special things for him. Maybe I shouldn't have."

Mark's eyebrows raised.

"Four nights a week Marie came home late. Tim would come home from work and go straight to his office, and we were supposed to leave him alone. But the kids missed him so much they would find ways to be loud or sneak in there. I found out they all love peanut butter, so I'd come up with weird little snacks for him and the kids when he came home from work, and work peanut butter into it each time. Things like that. The kids thought it was funny, and it was something they could share together. Then he'd work until seven o'clock when Marie came home."

Should she have kept more distance between Tim and herself? Her mind whirled through memories, and the confrontation with Tim came rushing back to her. "He said I'd ruined everything," Nic added. "I'd ruined Christmas for the kids."

Mark nodded and set down his glass. His face was drawn in sadness. "I'm sorry, Nic."

She looked up at him, trying hard to keep the tears from falling. "I didn't get to say good-bye. He took them out of the house while I packed, told me to be gone before he got back. I had Christmas presents for them, but I figured he'd throw them out." There was no stopping the tears now. "I didn't know what to do. I hid them in the basement closet. They loved hiding there when we played hide-and-seek. What if they find the presents, open them, and then get in trouble? And what did he say to them about me? Should I have told Marie?" She sobbed and he put his arms around her.

He stroked her hair as she cried all over his beautiful

tweed coat. But part of what she felt was a sense of relief. It wasn't long before she pulled herself together, snuffling and using the edge of a nearby towel to wipe off his jacket. That made him smile, and then his smile faded, but he didn't look away. It was the same soul-searching look he'd given her before, when they'd been sitting at the breakfast bar, right before she thought he might try to kiss her. She knew that he wasn't considering kissing her now. She was a mess. Maybe she was reading too much into that look. And his kindness. "I didn't mean to dump this all on you," she said.

He took a deep breath. "Do you think he's going to be vindictive?"

Nic remembered the way Tim Gordon had leaned over her where she sat trapped in her chair, jabbing his finger into her face. "You self-righteous little tease," he'd said. "Do you think you can break me?" She'd been afraid he was going to try to strike her.

"I don't know," Nic replied. "He threatened me. But that was in the heat of the moment."

Mark's eyes narrowed. "He threatened you?"

"I don't think anything will come of it. I'm just not his best friend."

"Don't underestimate this, Nic. You hold his reputation in your hands. And he sounds like a man who cares a lot about appearances. And himself."

Nic shrugged that off. "As if anyone would believe me. I'm not a threat to him. I don't even think I'm going back to Missoula. My best friend moved to Idaho, my job is done, I'm not going back to school—everything is up in the air."

Mark started to say something, but he clamped his mouth shut.

"What?" Nic asked.

"Nothing. Some other time."

"Time. We've got to get going. Hold on, let me wash the mascara off my face."

She left to freshen her makeup. When she finished, she found him hanging up the phone. He took both glasses of wine in one hand and opened the door for her with the other. From behind her, she heard him say, "I meant to tell you, you look nice tonight, Nic."

"So do you," she said as brightly as she could. More compliments? He was probably just trying to get her to cheer up so she'd stop sobbing like a baby.

Tracie and Melly were waiting by the entrance to the restaurant. Tracie looked stylish in a colorful ponté dress and high-heeled boots, and Melly looked adorable in a dress that was colored the same dark magenta as part of her mother's dress. "You look just like your mommy," Mark said. Melly glowed.

Nic noticed the dark circles under Melly's eyes. And Tracie's. She thought about working nights and being a mom during the day and wondered how Tracie managed.

Tracie pointed at the two glasses of wine Mark was carrying. "A two-fisted drinker, eh?"

"We got an early start."

"You did a bad job of it," she teased. Both glasses were still full.

"Your glass is on me. As is dinner."

"Mark…"

He frowned. "My treat, ladies. For all three of you. I

dare you to find a luckier guy here. And by here, I mean in all of Montana."

Tracie rolled her eyes, but she grinned. Nic found out that Mark had called Tracie from the room to invite her and made sure they had a table of their own. He'd asked for one tucked into a corner, near a window. From there they saw the last blue of twilight on the snow outside, and by candlelight Melly regaled them with the scary tale of a ride up the ski lift and steep descent down. Everyone agreed she was going to make an excellent skier and that growing a couple inches taller would help.

The restaurant was full of the patrons of the Alhambra Hotel, including many Vangs, Vang in-laws, and friends. Nic spotted Chris and Lauren, Jim and Meredith, and another couple sitting at one table. "They must be Jim's friends," she said. "We didn't meet their kids after all."

"So tonight is the big movie night," Tracie said. "I guess everyone is meeting in a conference room. We're supposed to bring blankets and pillows. That's a fun idea."

"Lauren's great about that sort of thing. And I bet you she has at least two backup plans for whatever might go wrong," Nic said. It was a fine line, being proud of her sister and wishing she wouldn't try to take on so much.

"As long as the kettle corn comes through, I can't imagine anything will go wrong," Mark said.

"Kettle corn?" Melly said, brightening.

Everyone's meal arrived soon after, including homemade macaroni and cheese for Melly. She ate quickly and faded almost immediately after that. Tracie offered her lap, and Melly buried her face against Tracie's shoulder and draped her arms around her neck.

"I heard you're a nanny now," Tracie said.

"I was. I quit."

"Why's that?"

Mark gave Nic a sympathetic look. "Mind if I answer?" he asked, and Nic nodded thankfully. "The dad made a pass at her."

"Ugh," Tracie said, disgust showing on her face. "That's awful. I hope you slapped him."

Tracie would have done just that, Nic thought. "No, sorry." If Tim hadn't seemed so angry, she might have.

"What a jerk," Tracie said. "His poor wife. And those poor kids. I bet they're missing you."

That thought made Nic's heart hurt. She didn't want them to miss her, but she didn't want them to forget her either.

"Is it hard, leaving them?" Tracie asked. She looked down at Melly, who was slumping in her arms, evidently asleep. "I think I'd get so attached. I had a friend in Billings who was a teacher, and she spent about a week crying at the end of every school year."

"Yeah. I've been pretty whiny." Nic smoothed the napkin across her lap.

"You have every right," Tracie said. "And I bet you're mad too. It's not fair that you've lost your job because he's a jerk."

Self-righteous little tease. Do you think you can break me? Was she deluding herself by thinking it was his fault alone? Maybe he was right. True, she'd never liked him much, but maybe she'd acted as if she had.

She remembered swimming with Mark, the way he'd put his arms around her, the way he'd—maybe—almost kissed her in the hotel room. Was she the kind of girl who sent off those signals? Had Elliot and Petra been hurt because of her?

"Hello, Tracie, Mark," Lauren said. "Was your dinner as good as ours?"

"It was wonderful," Mark answered, and Tracie nodded.

Lauren put a hand on Nic's shoulder. "I need to ask you something." And she waited.

Nic froze. She knew Lauren wanted her to leave the table, to speak to her alone, but she'd had enough confrontations for the day, so she played dumb. "What is it?" she asked.

Lauren gave her a pointed look that Nic knew meant "Fine, have it your way." Then she said, "Can you think of any reason the police would call me about you?"

"No," Nic said. "Are you sure they called about me?"

"Yes. They called my cell phone and wanted to know if you were with me."

"Which police, Alhambra?" Mark asked.

Lauren frowned and hesitated before answering him. "Missoula."

Nic tried to quell her anxiety. Had something happened to the Gordon family? Had something happened to the kids?

"What did they say?" she asked.

"They just said they were having trouble contacting you. I asked if it was an emergency, and they said no and wished me a Merry Christmas."

Nic took a deep breath. It couldn't be urgent. She wondered—had Marie found out? Had someone else received unwanted attention from Tim? But adultery wasn't illegal. It was immoral. And so very destructive.

"My cell phone has been off all this time. I should charge it back up."

"Doesn't matter now," Mark said. "If it were important they would have called you here at the hotel." That was a good point, and it comforted Nic. "You probably won't find out what it's about until after Christmas, if they decide to call you at all."

Nic nodded.

"I guess we'll see," Lauren said. "I'd better get back to my table. Let me know, please, Nic." There was a trace of condescension in that order.

The table was still after Lauren left.

Then Tracie said, "I always wanted a sister." She looked at Nic with a wry smile. "But maybe not a big sister."

"She did let me borrow her clothes," Nic offered.

"There is that. But the truth is, I liked being an only child. And speaking of that, Melly and I might do our own little movie night in our room. What do you think, Melly?"

Melly mumbled something unintelligible, and Tracie smiled. "Thank you for dinner, Mark. And Nic, if you end up on the run you can hide out at my place. A friend who also happens to be a nanny would be my dream roommate, even if you are an outlaw."

With Melly in her arms, Tracie stood with the expert strength of a loving mom and, with the tips of her fingers, waved good-bye with one hand.

"I like her," Nic said.

"Me too. Cole's an idiot."

"What happened?"

"I'll leave that for her to tell you sometime. I can say one thing, though. Drugs."

Nic sighed. She'd lost a couple high school friends to drugs. She'd never seen anyone she knew come back from drug addiction, but she could pray just the same. She tried to remember Cole and pictured a thin, tall man with a trendy haircut and colorful suits. He looked like a go-getter, a professional with big ambitions. Just like Chris and Jim. It was Mark who stood out among them. Not because he wasn't ambitious but because he had a peace about him. Maybe if Cole had that peace, he wouldn't need the drugs.

She soaked that peace in now, in silence. Lauren's words about the police had unsettled her, although she knew there was no need for worry. It helped that Mark seemed still and calm and that he looked at her with warmth in his eyes.

"It is my humble opinion that there isn't a single kid who will make it through a showing of *It's a Wonderful Life* tonight. And not many adults either," he said.

"I'd better go, just to support Lauren."

"It's Christmas Eve. If you had your choice, where would you be tonight?"

At their old home, she thought. The one Dad sold when she was eighteen, just after Mom died. She wanted that even more than being with Petra and Elliot. "I don't know. I haven't celebrated Christmas alone, ever. I'm usually working."

"You aren't alone," Mark said.

There was no trace of a smile when he said that, and his intensity made her squirm, so she teased him. "Who says I want to be with you?"

"It's me or the longest black-and-white movie ever made," he said.

"Bah humbug. And besides, they'll have kettle corn."

"I got the crackers. And I can steal kettle corn."

"Maybe the police are really after *you,*" she warned. "Cracker thief."

"Yes, and wait until you see my next caper," he said, looking like a rogue. "I just have a few details to work out." He caught the attention of their server and asked for the check.

"Would you like any dessert, Mr. Vang?" she asked.

"Good idea. I need two pieces of pie, one apple and one pumpkin, and a hunk of cheddar cheese to go." The server smiled and took the card he handed to her. "Thieves don't diet," he said to Nic.

I've missed you so much. She tried not to think that way, but there it was again. She placed her fingers on the base of her wine glass and rotated it around and around.

"You don't trust me," Mark said.

Was it written on her face?

"And I earned your mistrust," he added. "But I'm glad that you're here with me now. It's a blessing, and I'm thankful."

A blessing? She'd never considered herself a blessing to anyone. More of a liability. And lately she'd been a teary mess. She glanced up at the tiny lights that decorated the large windows of the restaurant. She hadn't noticed any of that, not the lights or the log walls or the view of the lights of Alhambra behind her, from dining here the day before.

Already her mind felt clearer and her heart felt stronger. She would survive losing Petra and Elliot, who were never really hers at all. Being with other kids helped. She'd have to remember that if she took another nanny job. And being with Mark helped. But that option wouldn't be around for her anymore.

Unless she moved to Glendive with Tracie. What a ridiculous idea. Two broke women and a child, all living down the road from her ex-boyfriend.

"Do you have your cross-country skis with you?" Mark asked. "We're going to need them. And ski poles. And something we could carve. Wait, do you have any clay?"

She eyed him carefully. "Why?"

"You do, don't you? Awesome." Mark chuckled.

"I have Play-Doh." It was one of her Boredom Bag staples.

"That stuff doesn't dry very fast. We'll have to hope the snow freezes it."

The server came back with the bill and a box, and Mark added a tip to the receipt and set it aside. "Let's see. We need hay. Where can we get some of that?"

"Hay?"

"For the reindeer."

She couldn't tell how much of what Mark was saying was teasing and how much pointed toward some unknown plan. "Hay? For flying reindeer? Everyone knows that reindeer eat reindeer food."

"What's that?"

"Oats and glitter. Also known as magic flying dust."

He stared at her. "That's genius. You're going to be a great mom, Nicole Benedict."

She held up her hand. "It wasn't my idea. Elliot's preschool teacher sent him home with a bag of it to scatter in his yard. And being a great mom takes a lot more than reindeer food."

He tapped his finger against his chin. "We also need ice skates. The awesome thing about you being homeless is that you probably have your ice skates with you."

"Yes. And that's not funny."

"Well, I don't have any, but I know where I can get some. I bet Chris has his."

"Chris skates?"

"Not unless there's a hockey puck involved, but I'd be willing to bet you my slice of pie that Lauren made him bring them just in case."

Nic giggled. "True. And it might be good for them, going for a romantic nighttime skate."

"Except the pond is closed to skating after dark."

"Rats."

"Then we're in agreement?" he asked, holding out his hand for a shake. She didn't budge. "Trust me," he said.

She reached out and shook his hand. It was as if her hand had moved by itself while her mind was still trying to sort things out.

"Good," he said. "You go up to the room and get our coats and my car keys. I'm going to take care of the difficult part myself."

"What's that?"

He glanced back at Lauren's table. The three men were deep in conversation, and one of them was writing with a stylus on a tablet. Two of the three women were talking to each other, and that left Lauren by herself, looking concerned. And glancing at her watch. "I'm going to steal Chris's key card."

"You what?"

“Shh. You trust me, remember?” He stood and politely pulled out Nic’s chair. “Meet me in the lobby in ten minutes.”

Across the room, Nic saw Lauren stand up and hurry out. It was almost time for the movie. Nic took a final sip of her wine as a delaying tactic, grabbed the dessert box, and slipped through the lobby and up the stairs.

She didn’t know what Mark was up to, but she did know Mark, and he’d never been mean. Whatever he was planning, she could trust him. Last Christmas Eve came to mind. He was *rarely* mean, she corrected herself.

It was Christmas Eve. That meant she had spent a few hours more than one year without him in her life, after spending one week less than a year with him. Was she crazy?

“I can handle this,” she said out loud. She was just passing time, just enjoying a situation she could do nothing about. And when it was over they would part ways as friends, something they hadn’t been for a long time. She could do friendship. She did it all the time, even with guys from school she suspected had an interest in her.

She pulled her warm ski parka from the back of a chair, gathered a few things from her Boredom Bag, and went into Mark’s room. His suitcase was sitting neatly on a luggage stand, but the bed was rumpled, with one of the blankets on the floor and one of the pillows in the corner of the room. It looked as if there had been four restless bears sleeping in that bed, not one man.

She found his coat draped over the suitcase. She squeezed the pockets, but to her hands they felt empty. Maybe his car keys weren’t on a chain, she thought. They would be easy to miss. So she looked in all his pockets. Nothing but a crumpled paper towel there, and a gas receipt.

She looked over the room, on the desk and nightstand, and anywhere on the floor where his keys might have fallen. Then she checked the living room, including under the towels and the couch cushions. Now what? She stared at his suitcase through narrowed eyes. She shouldn't. Or should she?

He would have just tossed his keys on top, she reasoned, so there wasn't much harm in peeking. It wasn't like she would have to rummage through his clothes. She opened the case, leaned over to peer inside, and a sparkle gave the keys away almost immediately.

But Mark's keys weren't the only thing that caught her eye. There was a small box inside his suitcase. It was made of thick, handcrafted paper and was wrapped in tiny gold ribbons with a glittering silver heart tied into the bow.

As ridiculously unlikely as it was, for one moment she wished it was for her. But another look made her think it was for him, and that he'd had it for a while. The tiny present's corners were crushed, and it had dirt smudges and even a water spot on the top. It looked as if it had been through a lot of handling but had never been opened. There was no way he'd give a gift that looked that way, so who had given it to him, and what had kept him from opening it?

But it wasn't any of her business. She took his keys, four keys attached to a well-worn green carabiner, and left his room. Mark wasn't in the lobby, but she thought she could hear him laughing inside the restaurant. She checked her watch; the movie would be starting now. She decided to wander around the lobby, looking at the decorations. The hotel Christmas tree had that fresh-cut pine scent, and antique glass ornaments hung on all its branches. Boughs draped with cream-colored ribbons draped along the top of the white-painted wainscoting. A fire was burning in the huge fireplace, swags of pine and candles lit the mantel, and golden stars dangled below, reflecting the light from the fire.

It was beautiful. Funny how Christmas finds me wherever I am, she thought. She'd been sure she'd miss it this year.

"Ready?" Mark asked from behind her.

She handed him his coat and keys and zipped up her coat, bracing for the first bitterly cold breath.

But the air was warmer than she'd expected. As they stepped off the hotel's front porch, she saw pine tops waving in the wind against an indigo sky. The wind merely swirled down below. The Alhambra Hotel's location in a timbered valley, backed against the hillside, gave it some shelter.

"Your car first. Come on, let's go," Mark said.

They retrieved her skates, cross-country skis, and boots. It took time and a lot of rearranging to find it all. She was about to shut the hatch door in the back when she thought of something.

That little cardboard box had started her thinking. What if he'd bought her something? Something like one of those balloon-covered stress balls. What would she give him in return?

"I'll meet you at your car," she said. "I want to grab something to wear tomorrow." As he trotted off, looking as excited as a child, she rummaged through a cardboard box she'd taken from the Gordons' recycling pile. She'd used it to pack odds and ends. Hidden beneath everything else inside was a tiny box with ridiculously girly decorations on it. It was small and inexpensive, and as a child it had been such a treasure. She opened the lid, and a miniature princess ice skater figurine stood and turned. But she only moved enough to play two notes, and they were whisked away by the wind. It had been a long time since Nic had wound the brass key.

There was a secret compartment in the bottom of the music box. It held her mother's pin, the same one she'd worn on her wedding day. There was a rhinestone rose pendant on a chain. The metal was cheap and now hopelessly tarnished, but it had been her favorite gift from Lauren. And there was a note from her father: "I'm proud of you." He'd attached it to her report card, fourth grade.

And there was one more thing. A simple cross made from hand-forged nails and bound together by solder and leather thongs. She couldn't be certain, but it was as close as she could come to the one Mrs. Vang had given to Mark. He'd lost it when they were camping in Yellowstone with some college friends, and he'd regretted it. She'd replaced the chain it came on with a leather cord to match the cross. She'd woven the cord herself after studying instructional videos online.

It was supposed to be his Christmas present last year. She'd tucked it away, out of sight and, until now, mostly out of mind. He'd probably replaced the cross, although she hadn't seen one around his neck. Maybe it wasn't his taste anymore.

"Better than a stress ball," she said to no one, tucking it into a pocket and closing the Velcro flap safely over it.

Then she hid the music box as best she could, closed up the Subaru, and went to find out what silliness Mark was up to.

He was sitting inside the SUV with the engine running. Her skis were propped up against his hood. She climbed into the passenger-side seat. "Where's the outfit you were getting?"

She shrugged. "Couldn't find it."

He was examining the end of a ski pole. "Did you bring the Play-Doh?"

She handed over a little yellow tub filled with brilliantly blue clay.

"Excellent." It was old and had often been used, so it was difficult to work. He divided it in half and handed half back to her. Then he formed the clay into a small pear shape, used a pencil from his dashboard to make a crease down the center, and made some other small changes. Then he held it up for her to examine.

"It's a blue pear? With the core cut out?"

He shook his head. "Nic, where is your Christmas spirit? It's obviously a miniature reindeer hoof." He skewered it onto the bottom of the ski pole and wrapped some string around it to keep it attached. "You'll have to be careful with it," he said.

"Me?"

"Well, your ski boots won't fit me. Here, you make the next one."

She wanted to ask him what his project was, but she was enjoying the silliness of it all. She followed his lead and created something she hoped was reindeer-like.

"Now the reindeer food." He pulled out four packets of instant oatmeal. "With cinnamon and raisins."

"Where did you get those?"

"The kitchen. It's amazing what you can get when you ask nicely. And when your parents booked half the hotel."

Nic pulled a plastic baggie of multicolored glitter from her pocket.

"Incredible," Mark said. "Why on earth did you have that?"

"Because Petra and I wrote a lot of letters, and Petra liked to put glitter inside hers."

"To drive the recipients insane?"

"She's seven. She's all things magic fairy princess."

Mark sighed. She thought he was going to say something like "I'm sorry" or "You must miss her," but he didn't. And she was grateful. He pocketed the oatmeal and the glitter. "I think we're ready. We have to go around and come in from the road side, though. It's the only place without tracks."

"You're speaking as if I know what you're up to. I don't."

"It's for your own good. If we get caught, you can plead innocence. You carry the boots and the skis, I'll carry the poles and skates."

She followed him across the parking lot, the century-and-a-half-old Alhambra glittering among the pine trees to her left.

She loved the wraparound porch of the old building. From here she could see the timber-framed extension where the restaurant was. There were so many windows the restaurant looked like a conservatory. There were a few smaller structures to the northeast and the blue glow of the indoor pool. She could also see the lighted steam from the outdoor pool rising to swirl around the pine trees.

The moon was rising, painting the tops of the snowy mountains and hills a silvery blue. They walked down the road by its light, and when a car pulled up toward the parking lot, they ducked into the woods like guilty children, laughing. They continued onto the frontage road, which ran up along the west side of the Alhambra. Here the pines surrounded the pond, and Mark gazed up at them.

"I have to find a good landing place for the sleigh. He'd be coming down right through here, I think. You'd better put your skis on. The problem is, I'd like the tracks to start off the road a bit."

So he was making sleigh tracks. "I could climb on that retaining wall and jump for it."

"If you fall you'll look make it look like Santa had a terrible accident."

She glowered at him. "It's a two-foot jump."

"On skis."

"Watch me." She climbed onto the wall, put on the cross-country skis, and balanced there. "Okay, jumping in skis is hard."

"You can do it!" he cheered in a loud whisper. "Ni-cole! Ni-cole!"

Nic balanced herself, rehearsed the landing in her mind, and jumped. She didn't make it as far as she'd hoped, but she stuck the landing like an Olympic ski jumper. Mark climbed on to the wall and handed her a ski pole. "Here's the first one."

"Why do we need two?"

"They have right and left feet."

"What's the difference?" Nic asked. They exchanged a confused look, and she started laughing again, trying to muffle the sound in the sleeve of her coat. "This is ridiculous."

"Yes, yes it is. Now you're on your own. I'm going to go around and meet you at the edge of the pond. Make sure you ski a couple feet before you start making prints, and remember, there's eight of them. Plus Rudolph. So nine reindeer times four feet, with an average stride length of about—"

"Go away," she ordered.

Now that she knew what they were doing, she did it well. She made sure her feet stayed the same distance apart, inching forward and pressing the ski pole "hoof" into the snow between the tracks. She tried to make it look random but not so cluttered that someone wouldn't be able to see the individual tracks. She kept an eye on the route through to the pond, but there was no one to ask what she was doing. It was Christmas Eve, after all.

She got to the edge of the pond just as Mark was making his way across the ice, one ski pole in one hand, her boots in the other, and two sets of ice skates draped over his shoulders. There was a small mound where the snow had been plowed off the pond, and she skied up and over the berm and onto the ice.

"Quick, change into your ice skates before anyone sees us," he said. He dropped everything to the ground, careful to set her boots upright. As soon as her ski boots were off, he gathered them, the poles, and her skis and took off at an awkward jog. "Be right back," he said over his shoulder.

She had taken the kids skating three times already this winter. She wasn't an expert skater, but she could get around on the ice. The ice was lumpy and a little rough from the warm wind, but skating was skating, and she always enjoyed it. She carried their things over to the other edge of the pond. Mark jogged up, out of breath and minus all the other equipment.

He put on Chris's hockey skates and stood on the ice, arms outstretched and a little unsteady. "It's been a while," he said. He reached for her and placed his hands on her shoulder, pushing her backward as he did. "Sorry." His skates skittered across the ice and his ankles shook.

"It'll come back to you," she encouraged. "I remember you used to be a great skater."

"We should have done this more," he said. "I was great, huh? Something like… this?"

He grabbed her right hand, slipped his left hand onto her left hip, and pushed out into a perfect glide. Laughing, she let him turn her forward and then backward again and into his embrace. "Shame on you, teasing me like that. And here I was trying to be polite about what a horrible skater you'd become."

They chased each other for a while and compared rusty skating skills. He tried a spin and landed so hard he lay spread-eagled on the ice for a while, moaning quietly. She did a passable spin, but when it came to racing, he left her in a shower of ice shavings.

He took her in his arms once more, swept her around the edge of the pond, then slowed down a little, weaving here and there to what felt to Nic like a waltz. "You have a song in your head," she said.

"I do," he said, and he began to sing it out loud.

. . .

It came upon the midnight clear,
That glorious song of old,
From angels bending near the earth,
To touch their harps of gold:
"Peace on the earth, goodwill to men,
From heaven's all-gracious King."
The world in solemn stillness lay,
To hear the angels sing.

The only accompaniment to his low, resonant voice was the high whisper of the wind in the treetops. She looked up toward the sound. Stars were scattered across the moonlit sky. As he skated her across the ice, it felt like she was flying through the night.

Nic loved the next verse and sang it with him.

Still through the cloven skies they come,
With peaceful wings unfurled,
And still their heavenly music floats
O'er all the weary world;
Above its sad and lowly plains,
They bend on hovering wing,
And ever o'er its Babel sounds
The blessed angels sing.

She loved the thought of angels singing over her, all her life, until the time she would be able to sing along. Her and her mother, who loved to sing.

Mark sang on alone through the next sad verses,

which spoke of the discord on earth, so busy with strife no one stops to listen to the angels' song. The lyrics called for hope in the face of struggle. She couldn't help but sing the last verse with him.

For lo! the days are hastening on,
By prophet bards foretold,
When with the ever-circling years
Comes round the age of gold
When peace shall over all the earth
Its ancient splendors fling,
And the whole world give back the song
Which now the angels sing.

He tucked her hand against his chest and pulled her closer until they drifted to a stop. She rested her cheek against his shoulder. That same coat, that same smell, the same warm, safe place.

How amazing it was to imagine just for a moment that it wouldn't end. That the last year had never happened. But the last year had changed so much in her life. Would she trade that away? She closed her eyes and let the wind brush strands of her hair across her face. No, things had been as they should have been. It had been hard. But there was a higher plan.

"I missed you," he said softly. "Every day."

She let the sweet, sad tone of his voice and the rush of the winter wind fall all around her. She held her breath.

"I wanted to tell you when I saw you at the wedding, Nic."

She remembered that stressful day, one week after they'd broken up. She'd been proud of her performance, so cheerful and disinterested, unshakably strong. He'd listened to her with a steady gaze and unreadable, stiff smile. How could he have been so cold?

But now she could hear something in his voice. The low strain of a hurting heart. "I wanted to tell you then," he said.

She wished he would stop talking. She didn't want to be reminded. He had left her. He had made his decision. And if he missed her, it didn't take the edge off the pain. It only made it worse.

They heard voices, and Mark rushed her over into the shadows, where they stood and waited. A couple walked by, but they were oblivious to anything going on around them. As soon as the front door of the Alhambra Hotel closed behind them, Mark said, "Quick, the reindeer food, before we get kicked off the pond." He led her to a spot near the sleigh tracks and ripped open the paper packages and scattered the oatmeal here and there. He handed Nic the glitter again, and she scattered that over the oatmeal.

"You know we're going to have to clean this up tomorrow," she said.

"Not if it snows. Then the plows will get what the mice don't eat."

"What, you don't believe in flying reindeer?"

He grinned at her. "On a night like tonight I do. Come on, it's getting late. Melly first, okay?"

She was still trying to piece together what his plan was, but she was content to follow, taking off her skates as he did, and going inside. She and Mark hurried down the quiet hallway that led to the hotel rooms on the first floor.

He stood in front of a door, arm raised. "I hope this is the right one," he said.

"Mark, we should double-check."

"I'm joking." He knocked softly.

She elbowed him in the ribs. But he held his position, making a funny face into the peephole. The lock slid open quietly, and Tracie stuck her head out. "What on earth?" She spotted Nic and added, "What has he done now?"

"Get your coat and boots on. Get Melly all bundled up, we're going outside."

Tracie shook her head, made a funny face, and let him in. She put a coat over her Hello Kitty pajamas and gently stroked Melly's face. The girl was asleep in the bed already. "Is it Santa?" she asked sleepily.

"It might be," Mark said, walking inside. Nic held the door while he helped get a coat on Melly, and a hat, and boots. That was when Nic noticed she was wearing pajamas to match her mother. It made Nic feel happy and miss her mom all at once. When Melly was wrapped up, Mark lifted her and carried her into the hall.

"He's crazy," Tracie said as she walked past Nic. "Lucky for you, he's crazy in a good way."

Mark walked right up to the front desk. "Do you have a flashlight I can borrow?"

"Yes, Mr. Vang, hold on just a minute." The man disappeared into a back office and came back with just what they needed, no questions asked. Nic shook her head.

What a different world he'd grown up in, she thought. And she had once thought they had so much in common. She'd probably only seen what she wanted to see.

As soon as they made it outside, Melly groaned. "It's cold."

"I know, sweetheart. But Nic and I saw something, and I need your expertise."

"What?"

He set her down on her feet. "Here's what happened. Nic and I put out some reindeer food. We went for a walk, and when we came back, most of the food was gone. We think that Dasher, Dancer, Rudolph, and all the others dropped by to refuel."

"Where?" Melly asked, looking up at the sky.

"They're gone now. It's not the time for our presents to come yet. But I don't know for sure, I need you to look." He picked her up again and carried her out onto the ice. "Now be careful, but—"

"Reindeer food!" she squealed.

Mark shot Nic a conspiratorial glance.

It took a little maneuvering to get Melly over to the tracks, but it didn't take long for her to piece it together. The tracks led straight to the pond, where the reindeer had stopped for a snack. "You should have left cookies too," she scolded. Then she jumped up and down. "They were here!"

"What do you think we should do?" Mark asked.

"Can we show the other kids?"

"I think that's very kind of you," Mark said, and they all tromped back inside and into the very quiet conference room. It was the final scene of the movie. Jimmy Stewart was in the arms of his wife, and Clarence was about to hear a bell ring for him.

Mark flicked on the light.

Nic winced and a collective groan rose from the group.

"You guys," Melly said, stomping her snow-covered

boots, "Santa was here."

Mark was right, most of the kids had been asleep, but they started waking each other up after that. Tegan stood up first. "What? Where?"

"Grab your blankets and we'll show you," Mark said.

Nic gauged the expressions of the adults in the room. There were a few irritated faces, but Melly's enthusiasm was irresistible, and soon the whole crew was headed out to the pond. Mark handed the flashlight to Melly, and she told everyone the story of how Mark and Nic had gotten Santa to land on the ice. A few of the parents pulled out cell phones to snap pictures in the dark.

Nic caught sight of Lauren. She was standing a few steps back from the others, looking cold in her white turtleneck. Nic walked over to apologize for pulling the plug on the movie before the Christmas tree bell rang, but Lauren's attention was on someone standing behind Nic.

Mrs. Vang had come out on the ice. She was wearing a long wool coat. As she came closer, Nic realized it was houndstooth plaid, probably black and white, but for one terrible moment it looked like a Dalmatian coat à la Cruella De Vil. She stifled a laugh.

Mrs. Vang was intimidating, but she wasn't mean. She carefully tiptoed over and put a hand on Lauren's arm. "I just wanted to thank you for everything you've done, Lauren," she said. "You pulled it all off without a hitch."

"Well, the holiday isn't over yet, but thank you." Even by moonlight Nic could see how pleased Lauren was. Nic heard footsteps approaching and wondered if Mr. Vang was coming, but when she turned, she saw Mark instead.

"Everyone has told me what a lovely time they've had," Mrs. Vang continued. She lowered her voice. "And now this. What a clever idea. You've added just the right amount of Christmas magic by having Santa visit."

The smile died on Lauren's face. She started to speak, but Mark interrupted.

"Hello, Mom," he said, giving Mrs. Vang a kiss on the cheek. He continued around his mother and put an arm on Lauren's shoulders. "I think you're right, Mom. It's been a good Christmas. Thanks for all your time, Lauren."

Eddie let out a wail. "Santa came and didn't leave me any presents!"

Mrs. Vang chuckled and carefully edged back toward the shore. Mark let go of Lauren and took Nic by the elbow, walking away before Lauren could react one way or another to Mark's intervention.

Eddie was still yelling, but then Melly took him by his shoulders and said firmly, "He's coming back. But if he doesn't leave you any presents, that's because you've got a family and they take care of you. He's got to give presents to kids that don't. Remember, it's Jesus' birthday. He wants everyone to get a present."

Nic glanced at Tracie, who had pressed her hands to her face.

"Melly's got this Christmas thing down," Mark whispered in Nic's ear.

The kids stomped through the snow to examine where the reindeer and sleigh tracks began, obliterating them as they went. Everyone got cold and wet, and eventually the parents dragged them back inside. Before she left, Tracie came over, looked at Nic and Mark, and said, "I love you guys." Then she ushered her little girl back to her room.

Nic was shivering. The wind had picked up, and now it had a bitter edge to it. It smelled like snow. When she looked up, she saw that the clouds had moved in and the stars were gone. "Time to go in," Mark said. "Want to watch *It's A Wonderful Life?*"

"Yes. I love that movie."

He moaned. He put his arm around her shoulders and walked with her to the hotel. With every step she thought she should move away from his touch, but it felt so warm and comforting. It was just a friendly gesture, she reasoned.

The lobby lights had been turned down, leaving only the Christmas decorations shining. He led her over to the fireplace, and she gratefully let its warmth soak in. Mark sat down in a chair, and she heard a *thunk* as his skates hit the floor.

"You need to get those back to Chris," she said.

Mark pressed his palm to his forehead. "Oh, I forgot his key card. That's what I need to get back to him. I told him I needed to borrow some stuff to wear. I know, it was kind of vague. I'm pretty sure he's still in the bar. There must be some serious deal making going on to be up this late on Christmas Eve."

Nic picked up her skates and dangled them in her hand. "I'll meet you in the room, okay?"

She started for the stairs, but she couldn't help but think about Lauren. She wouldn't like taking credit for the Santa visit. But she deserved the praise, and Nic wanted to tell her that. She checked the conference room, but it was empty. So she walked down the hall toward the next wing, where the pool-view rooms were. She wondered if she'd remember which room was Lauren's. Was it 116? 117?

She heard her name and stopped just before turning the corner.

"He's the problem, not Nic. Everything bad that has happened has been because of your brother. He toyed with her." It was Lauren, sounding distraught.

"Don't even," a lower voice growled. Chris. "He had a good reason to end it. And look at his life since he dated her. Dropped out of school, working as a custodian. How much worse can it get? Do you realize how much better his life was before he met her? But it's not about that. You know we don't have the money to bail her out of whatever mess she's gotten into now. Or him."

Nic was frozen. She knew she should turn and leave, but she couldn't. Bail her out of what? She had never asked for anything from them.

"She was not the kind of girl who would, would"—Lauren's voice lowered to a hiss—"get in trouble with the law before she dated *him*."

What? She wasn't in trouble with the law. Though she still had no idea why the police had called.

"Chris, I don't want to get sidetracked talking about them. I don't want to have to wait to see what happens with her, or with your new partnership. We don't need the fancy cars or the big house."

"You're naive."

"I want a family, Chris."

"Now of all times? Besides, you have one. And she's a toxic mess."

Nic knew Mark was coming up behind her. She knew the swish of his coat as his arms swung, and she heard his steps falter when he heard his brother's voice.

"Nic is the kind of girl who seems innocent, but when

you get to know her, you find out she's broken. And anyone who tries to save her will end up broken too."

Self-righteous little tease. Do you think you can break me?

She felt Mark's hand close around her arm. She knew he would pull her away from here, where she had no right to be.

But he didn't. He took a firm hold and held her tight beside him as he walked forward, around the corner and into sight.

Nic kept her eyes down. Mark reached up with one hand and took the skates from where they hung on his shoulder and handed them to Chris. "Borrowed your skates," he said. Then he dug into his pocket and handed over the key card. "Thanks."

The moment they had turned out of sight again he let go of Niç and left her there as he wheeled around. His voice was low, but she heard his words from around the corner. "Whatever difficulty you guys are facing, you need to fix it. Together. With God. Because finger-pointing isn't working for you. Or anyone else."

He came back around the corner and took her elbow again. She pulled away. He just reached for her hand and held it tight all the way to their suite.

"Not the Christmas Eve I was hoping for," he said. "I'd rather watch the movie." He cut her a glance. "Too soon to joke?"

She shook her head. She knew he was trying to make her feel better, but her mind was full of the echoes of voices she didn't want to hear. She sat down on the couch, still wearing her big coat and still feeling cold.

Mark sat down on the coffee table and leaned forward with his hands clasped, elbows on his knees. "Are you okay? That was rough. And although I'm not in the mood to defend him right now, I've got to say that Chris didn't sound like himself. I know he didn't mean everything he said. Remember, he's the one that fixed us up in the first place."

That was before he got to know me, Nic thought. "Mark, what has the last year of your life been like?"

He contemplated her for a while. "I didn't end up broken, if that's what you mean," he said.

She hated that he knew what she was trying to get at. She looked over at the door and wondered where she'd go if she left right now.

"The first thing I did when we broke up was quit school."

"Why?"

"That's what everyone asked. I like being outdoors, games, all that physical stuff. And I like serving people. It seemed like being a physical therapist was the best job for me. It was even a tiny bit like being the doctor Mom wanted me to be. The only problem was, I hated it. Everything about it."

"I didn't know that," she said. She knew it had been difficult for him, even boring, but she'd thought he wanted the career.

"I never told you because you were one of the reasons I was doing it."

Nic crossed her arms. "What do you mean?"

"I mean, I was trying to be a particular person. Stable, a good provider, a respectable job. That's how Vang men are. They provide." He ran his fingers through his hair. "I quit, and I got a job as an attendant at a KOA in New Mexico. I lived out of my Dodge, and I enrolled in an online university program. A couple months later I had a Certificate of Religious Counseling."

"I didn't know that," she said.

"No one knows, except for the pastors at my church. I went to a pastor's retreat that spring, that's where I met the pastor at my church. Next thing I know, I'm living in Glendive, working at the church, and earning a bachelor's degree in religious studies. If all goes well, I'll have that degree in another two years. Then I'm going for a master's."

He didn't try to explain or defend his plans, he just stated them with confidence. His hands were still clasped together. She saw the clarity in his blue eyes.

"You love it."

"I do. It's everything I love. I get to serve. I get to be active. And I get to be goofy. I have my eye on a couple career paths, all related to youth ministries, but I might also stay where I am and help grow the church. I'll have to wait and see what God has planned for me."

"But Chris doesn't know. Or Jim, or your parents."

"I'm certain about what I'm doing, Nic. But I figure I owe them real progress before I spring yet another career change on them. I need at least a year at the seminary, maybe even more."

He spoke with quiet confidence, so much more than she ever remembered him having. She felt torn between being happy for him and feeling as if she'd been left behind. "I was holding you back."

"No, no way. I need you to understand that, Nic," he said, placing his hand on her knee. "I'm not saying you expected anything of me. I wasn't living up to who I wanted to be, not just for you and my family, but for God.

I knew I wasn't on the right track." He leaned back and shook his head. "Someday I'll tell you about all the strange things that happened to get me to that stupid KOA, which was run by a former Bible camp counselor." He shook his head.

"I needed to get away from all the voices in my head telling me who I should be and what I should be like, Nic. And when it all quieted down, I could hear God. And although I know you don't trust me, I also heard you. You always believed in me. I think you like the same things about me that God likes. That's hard to find. For anyone."

Nic rubbed her hands together. "Great. So I'm an excellent ex-girlfriend."

"No, you're an excellent whatever you're willing to be. Anything you want to be."

Nic didn't know what to do with that statement. Was he implying that he wanted her to be something more? She couldn't tell. It felt as if the ground beneath her was unstable. She didn't know what to read into his words, or Chris's, or Lauren's.

Or her mom's, for that matter. It hit her square in the chest. It wasn't Lauren she'd been trying to appease. It was as if Lauren was the gatekeeper for Mom. She was older; she'd known Mom longer and better. They even looked alike, with rounder faces and cuter noses than Nic's.

College, her music degree, all those things Lauren thought Mom had wanted for her. "Mom would be so proud of you. Mom would have loved to hear you play. Mom…"

It was true. Mom liked to listen to her practice. Mom liked to sing. But Nic also remembered her mother before high school orchestra performances, shaking her hands out so hard she bounced up and down in her seat. "I'm a nervous wreck," she'd say.

She could hear Lauren's words on Christmas Day a year ago. "I'm glad Mark is gone. You know Mom would want you to settle down with a man who can take good care of you. Someone like Chris." Nic blew out a lungful of air and felt her shoulders sag. What would it be like to drive her packed car to a KOA and sleep in the back for a season? Would it quiet the voices in her head?

But there were no supernatural signposts pointing her to do that. Or maybe there were. If God was trying to direct her path, was she missing the signs?

She glanced at Mark, conscious of how long she'd been sitting there, thinking.

"You look like you could use some dessert," he said.

"I think you're right."

Mark got the box out of the fridge and came over with two clean forks. He grabbed the remote control, sat down beside her, and watched the channel guide scroll on the TV screen as Nic crumbled cheese over her piece of pie.

"You sure you don't want the pumpkin?" he offered.

"I like what I like," she said.

"Aha! I knew it." The channel changed, and a familiar black-and-white movie appeared.

"It's on because so many people like it. Christmas is a good time to reflect on your life and the things that matter," she said.

"It's a movie about emotional abuse, bankruptcy, and attempted suicide."

She threw a piece of cheese at him.

He turned the guide back on, clicked on another channel, and suddenly they were on the nearly crashing *Polar*

Express. She teased him about watching cartoons, but soon they were both engrossed. She found herself silently cheering for the boy as Santa passed by just out of view. *Just have faith. Just believe.*

When the movie was over, she felt tired and satisfied. For a little while the rest of the world had backed off.

"So tomorrow—" she started.

"Will take care of itself," he said, nudging her shoulder with his. "Get some sleep. You've been yawning for the last half hour."

Nic felt as if there were things she should ask, or say, but he took her hand and pulled her to her feet. "Goodnight," he said firmly.

"Goodnight." She went to her room and looked out the window.

Snow was falling outside.

CHRISTMAS

It was dark. Why would anyone try to wake her in the middle of the night? The knock came again, and for how it felt, the pounding might as well have been directly on her head.

"It's Christmas, sleepyhead!" Mark called through the closed door.

"It's still Christmas Eve," she mumbled into the pillow. It was a wonderful pillow, fluffy but substantial, clean and crisp. She had no intention of leaving it.

The door opened. "Come on. I have breakfast. Just throw on a hoodie and come out here."

She pulled the covers down just far enough to see that Mark had already dressed in jeans and a hoodie. What was it with morning people? "Shh."

"Don't make me wake you up, Nic."

With the one eye that could see over the covers, she gave him a fierce glare. "Don't you dare."

"You have two minutes. Then I'm coming after you." He closed the door behind him.

"You are the worst Santa ever!" she yelled. Her room was freezing—no wonder the covers felt so good. Getting out from under them felt like jumping into ice water.

She put her coat on over her red plaid flannel pajama bottoms and her thermal top, grabbed her toothbrush, and went straight to the bathroom. When she was done brushing, she propped herself against the bathroom door and glowered at him. "It's too early for breakfast."

"Nope. The continental breakfast just opened. It's after 6:00 a.m."

"Ugh, 6:00? Are you crazy?"

But there were two plates full of waffles, eggs, and donuts, and two cups of coffee with candy canes in them. She tried not to smile at that. It was too early to give up her sleepy crankiness.

After a few syrupy bites of waffle and a sip of coffee, he asked about her favorite Christmas morning. She told him about the plastic blue pony with a long mane and tail and a glittery star on its rear end, and they laughed over the fact that she'd also gotten a keyboard. Which she refused to play. Years later the pony was long gone, but the keyboard had gotten her through three years of piano lessons.

Mark's favorite Christmas was the one when his father drove them up to a friend's cabin before dawn and they rode a zip line down the frozen mountainside. In the rush, Mark forgot one of his boots and had to do everything wearing one boot and one slipper.

He talked about the thematic Christmas ornaments each child got every year, which his brothers joked about relentlessly. Especially the "favorite book" year. No one was certain what the pink owl, ferret, and typewriter were supposed to represent. And yet all those ornaments were on each man's tree now. Mark said his were hanging on a three-foot-tall garage-sale purchase next to his futon in the church basement.

And Nic talked about the music. When she got older, Nic always had a new instrument to try out. One year Christmas fell right in the middle of Nic's trombone phase. But they all could sing, and nothing made her mother happier than having all her family under one roof. And often a few stragglers from the neighbors. "She was an early riser like you," Nic added, glaring at him.

"This is going to be a great Christmas for you." A shadow of doubt crossed his face. "I hope. I got you a present. I mean, I got it a while ago. I don't know what you're going to think about it."

She remembered the cross pendant in her pocket. Would he like it?

"I'll like it more if I get another cup of coffee," she said.

"I can get that for you," he offered, standing up.

"I'll go with you. I want to check out the donut collection." He grinned at her, and she innocently raised her hands. "What? It's Christmas."

The lobby was empty. There was no one at the front desk, and no one at the breakfast station set up outside the restaurant. They piled a plate high with green and red sparkled treats, and he poured more coffee. They were so engrossed in their task she hardly noticed the front doors open.

A cold breeze and a swirl of snow heralded the arrival of two police officers. She turned and looked at them, and her heart skipped a beat. Guilty conscience, she thought, although she had no idea what she had to feel guilty about. Her Mark daydreams were stupid, not illegal. Was it the toilet-paper roll she'd stolen from work at the car wash? Hers had run out and she hadn't had time to get more after work. They'd have mercy, right? She had brought back a roll to replace it. A much nicer roll too.

The police officers looked her way, exchanged a few words without taking their eyes off her, and walked over. One wore a polite smile and the other looked from her to Mark and back again.

"Nicole Benedict?"

Her heart was beating all the way up to her throat. "Yes?" she said. How did they know?

"That's good luck," he said. "My name is Officer Mike Stanton. This is Officer Washington. We're from the Alhambra Police Department. The Missoula PD asked if we could speak to you."

Missoula. It was about the Gordons. "Yes?" she said. Her throat was tight, her voice strangled, and her lips quivered as if she was about to cry. It was going to take more than deep-breathing exercises to calm her down this time. "Has something happened?"

"Well, that's what we're here to find out."

"On Christmas morning?" Mark asked.

"It's Christmas for us, too," Officer Stanton said. He smiled, but he didn't really look happy. "We're investigating a theft. Would you mind leaving the coffee here for a moment, Miss Benedict? We'd like to have a talk with you."

"Not without me," Mark said.

"Is this your boyfriend?" the other officer asked. He was younger, and he looked as if he expected them to draw a gun on him at any moment.

"No," she said. The younger man's eyebrows dropped just for a moment. Here she was standing in her pajamas with a man at six something in the morning and he supposedly wasn't her boyfriend. No wonder the officer looked dubious.

"I suppose he can listen in, but we aren't here to talk to you, Mr.—"

"Vang. Mark Vang." The way he said it had a James Bond feel to it, and Nic was so off-kilter she had to strangle down a nervous giggle.

When the older officer gestured to one of the small tables near the breakfast buffet, Nic noticed other guests coming their way. Luckily, their faces weren't familiar. She chose the table farthest from the hallway, for all the good it would do.

"What is this about?" Mark asked.

Officer Stanton gave him a gentle but disapproving smile, then pointedly turned to Nic. "You are employed by the Gordon family of Missoula, right?"

"I used to be. I quit." She had to count—had it only been four days? It felt longer. "Four days ago."

"On Monday?"

"No, Wednesday." She got the feeling he already knew that.

"And why did you leave your job?"

Nic felt her panic rising. Something was very, very wrong. The man was polite, but he was questioning her as if she had done something illegal. She swallowed, but it was as if the spit in her mouth was dry clay. She took a deep breath through her nose. "I quit," she repeated, her voice trembling. She couldn't get anything else out.

"And why did you quit?"

"Why are you asking?" Mark said.

"Mr. Vang, you are interrupting. I would like to have you here, you might have some information for us, but it would help if you would let Miss Benedict answer the questions I'm asking." Officer Stanton's expression was as neutral as his flat tone of voice. It was a warning.

"Mr. Gordon and I had a disagreement. So I quit."

"You seem quite nervous, Miss Benedict," Officer Stanton said. "Is there a problem?"

She could feel the cold sweat break out on her forehead. She didn't dare try to speak again.

After a several seconds of staring at her, Officer Stanton continued. "Mrs. Gordon contacted us, stating that a necklace was stolen from Mr. Gordon's office. Missoula police investigated, and Mr. Gordon stated that he had reason to believe you had stolen a diamond and ruby necklace of considerable value, a gift he had purchased for his wife. Do you know the necklace I'm talking about?"

Nic felt sick to her stomach. This was much worse than she had imagined. She nodded slowly. She knew of the necklace, but it hadn't been purchased for Marie.

"Do you have it?"

She shook her head, a tiny, nervous gesture. In the back of her mind she thought she must look just like Lauren. That made her glance toward the hallway. What if Lauren—or Chris?—saw her now. Already Ingrid was nearby, and she was looking at Nic. She turned away as soon as Nic met her eye.

"How do you know about the necklace?"

"He gave it to me." Her voice was a shaky shadow of itself now. The police noticed, of course.

"He gave it to you," Officer Stanton said, eyebrows raised. "He didn't mention that."

"I'm sure he didn't," Mark said.

Officer Stanton was about to make him leave, she was certain, so she spoke fast. After all, there was no mistaking where this was heading. "You'll want to search my things."

Stanton looked a little surprised. "Well, that might be helpful. I'm assuming you're going to tell me that you didn't take the necklace, even though Mr. Gordon offered it to you."

"No, I didn't. The last time I saw it, it was in his office." He'd thrown it against the bookshelf. She looked up. There was Jim, talking to Ingrid and glancing her way. "We should go to my room so you can search."

"Very well," Officer Stanton said.

Mark reached for her hand, but she wriggled out of his grasp. She didn't want him to feel the dampness there or the shaking. It was only a matter of time before he looked askance at her the same way the officers were. She led the way up the stairs. She slipped into the room, but not before she saw Jim's friends standing farther down the hallway.

Nic sat on the stool by the breakfast bar. Her whole body was shaking now, and she could smell her own sweat. She must have looked guilty beyond doubt. With this traitorous body, she had no chance of passing a polygraph. How much was the necklace worth? Thousands. Stealing it would be a felony.

Mark disappeared as the officers looked through the living room, under cushions, in the refrigerator. Had he gone to tell the others? To seek advice about what to do with her now that she was a suspect in a theft? But he came back quickly, her coffee in his hand. He set it down in front of her. "What is this about a necklace?" he asked her, his voice and eyes gentle.

Would he believe her?

Officer Stanton approached them, and as she looked up, she saw the other officer going into Mark's room. "That's not my room," she said.

"We will need to search it as well," Officer Stanton said.

She looked at Mark. "I'm sorry," she mouthed. She hadn't realized.

Mark shrugged. "Maybe they'll make the bed. It's a disaster."

She smiled, thinking of the strewn blanket and pillow. "It was." Now the officer would think she'd slept there. She tried to clarify, telling Mark, "I saw it yesterday, when I was searching for your keys." By the time she'd reached the last word, her voice was just a quavering whisper.

"Miss Benedict, it would help me if you would explain what went on with Mr. Gordon and the necklace."

There was something about the way Officer Stanton looked down on her that made Nic feel trapped. God, why is this happening to me? But there was nothing to say. Who would believe her over Tim Gordon?

"You need to tell him," Mark said.

Officer Stanton's eyes darted to Mark then back to her.

She shook her head. One tiny little shake. When Lauren did that, did she feel the same way? As if any movement more would make her explode with all the tension inside her?

I'm sorry, Lauren. I never realized.

Mark looked at the officer. “Nic has a pretty severe case of stage fright.”

“Stage fright,” Officer Stanton repeated.

“Anxiety attacks brought on in public situations.”

“This isn’t a stage, Mr. Vang.”

Mark sighed. “But her performance is in question, right?”

Officer Stanton seemed to consider that.

Behind him, the other officer moved to the bathroom. She wondered if he’d opened the little box in Mark’s suitcase. No doubt he had, and she wished she knew what he’d found. She didn’t think would ever tell her. After today, she’d be lucky if Mark ever spoke to her again.

They would need to search the car, she realized, and she was still wearing pajamas. “I would like to change clothes,” she said.

The officer nodded. “I’ll come with you to pick them out if you don’t mind.”

She went to her room, conscious and slightly angry as he watched her take out underwear, socks, warm leggings, and a tunic. She didn’t even ask. She just put her boots on top and handed the whole thing to him, turning away. He handed it back to her shortly.

“And I’ll need to search you,” he said.

Of course. She handed the coat to him, and he went through its many pockets. When he reached into the pocket on the left side, she remembered and gasped. He froze, staring at her. “Is there something in here I should know about?”

She looked over her shoulder. She couldn’t see Mark. “It’s a present,” she whispered. “Don’t let him know.”

Officer Stanton took out the cross pendant, stared at it

for a moment, then put it back. He set the coat on the bed. "I'll need to search your person."

She held out her arms. He was quick about it, but the thermal shirt and pajama bottoms didn't leave much room to hide things. When he was done, she was red in the face and couldn't say a word.

"You can change in the bathroom," the officer said.

She went in, closed the door, slid to the floor, and hugged her knees to her chest. Then she wiped her tears with some toilet paper and washed with a cool washcloth. Changing clothes was frustrating. She couldn't even stand on one leg to pull on the leggings without bracing herself, the shaking was so bad.

"Great Christmas," she whispered to the mirror, but her conscience caught her. There were people all over the world who would be harassed and jailed today. Some of them would be lost in a world of drugs. Others would be innocent but living in places without the due process of law. If she felt violated, how much worse did other people feel, at this very moment?

It wasn't about her having a nice day. It was about the birth of her Lord and Savior. And if this was what he wanted to happen today, she would make it through. He had a plan. That was all she needed to know.

When she came out, Officer Stanton was waiting to hand her coat back to her.

"My car is in the parking lot," she said. Officer Stanton looked concerned. Maybe he didn't want to go out into the bitter cold, she thought. Good. It was fine with her if he was as uncomfortable as she was. "You can stay here," she said to Mark, but he stood up and firmly took her hand.

"I'm right here," Mark said. He turned to face her, closed his eyes, and said softly, "Lord, please watch over us. We pray for wisdom and peace, knowing that You are God of justice. Amen." He leaned forward to give her a kiss on the forehead, and they left the room.

The officers followed her out. She didn't even bother to look into the faces that she passed. The way gossip traveled in families, everyone would know by now.

The air outside was still, and the coldest she'd felt all year. She put her mittens over her mouth in order to breathe properly. In the dim morning light across the parking lot, someone was unloading an industrial-grade snowblower from a truck that had a plow on the front. None of the snow had been removed yet, and only the first traces of dawn had touched the sky. It was beautiful.

The snow had to be at least six inches deep. She trudged out toward her car. It didn't look like much more than a small, snowy hill in the parking lot. She brushed the snow off the hatchback, and Mark helped, clearing the snow from above the doors. She unlocked it and opened the passenger-side door. Then she pulled out the blanket she kept for driving on snowy mornings, walked to the rear, and spread it out over the snow. "Please don't drop my things in the snow," she asked. "And be gentle with the instruments. They'll be brittle in this weather."

Her twelve string worried her. It shouldn't be in cold like this, but it was better to leave it alone now than bring it directly from this bitter cold into the warmth of the lodge.

Officer Stanton was definitely looking uncomfortable now, and his discomfort seemed to be about more than the weather. He opened the hatch and looked things over, then he went to the driver's side and explored the Subaru's cubby holes. The other officer took over, moving things from the back of the car to the blanket with a decent amount of care. It didn't take long for him to pull out the cardboard box. And then, beneath a jumble of photographs and mementos, he found the music box.

She sucked in her breath. He heard something rattle in the box, and it didn't take long for him to find her "secret" compartment. As his gloved fingers touched the tarnished chain, the slip of paper that had been folded and refolded so many times, tears came to her eyes.

"Miss Vang, I really think it's time you tell me what's going on here," Officer Stanton said. She hadn't even seen him walk over.

"You won't believe me." She felt Mark's hand on her shoulder.

"Try me," Officer Stanton said.

"Tim Gordon is a very influential man."

Officer Stanton tipped his head sideways. "Miss Benedict, I don't know Tim Gordon. And I really couldn't care less. I know every single soul in Alhambra, and if there's one thing I've learned, it's that nothing would surprise me about any of them."

Her throat closed, and she fought for breath, but she could only manage short gasps. "Come over here, Miss Benedict. I'd like you to sit down in your car. Why don't you start it and turn on the heat too? It's awfully cold out here."

She did as she asked, leaving the door open and her snowy boots on the ground. *You are God of justice,* Mark had prayed. It felt good to know that was true. It was also good to have Mark standing nearby. It took her longer than it should have, but she finally felt able to talk. "I was Petra and Elliot's nanny for almost a year. The Gordons are busy. Even when they're home."

"Did they treat you well, Miss Benedict?"

"Very. But Mr. Gordon made me uncomfortable." Should she have paid better attention to that feeling? "Then again, so do you, Officer Stanton."

The policeman grinned at that. "Fair enough. What happened to make you leave?"

"Mr. Gordon called me into his office. I'm… we're not allowed in there. He closed the door and told me he appreciated the work I was doing." She stopped, remembering how she had felt. "Said I had a gift for noticing the little things. And he said he had a little thing to give me. He handed me a long, red velvet box, and when I opened it, I saw the necklace."

"What did you do?"

"I said thank you. I was trying to be polite, but I thought it was ugly. It was gaudy and big and I just assumed it was costume jewelry. He wasn't very happy with my reaction. He got kind of upset and told me it was very valuable. He said how many karats of rubies and diamonds there were—a lot, I don't remember how many."

Officer Stanton nodded. "What did you do?"

"I told him I couldn't accept it."

"And what did he say?"

That made her heart quicken again. She stared down at her gloved hands. They were shaking. Even with the heat running full blast the air was so cold it bit right through to her fingers. "He said no one had to know he'd given it to me. That he just wanted to know it was touching my skin."

The last few words were just a whisper. She shook it off as best she could and sat up straighter. "I knew my job was over. I told him I didn't share his feelings, and that when he had time to think about it, he'd realize he'd made a mistake. I said I would be leaving as soon as Christmas was over. He took the box from my hands and threw it. It hit the big bookcase. I think it landed on his desk. I didn't look. I thought that if he would do that to an expensive necklace, I wasn't sure what he would do to me."

"And what happened then, Miss Benedict?"

That she remembered word for word. She told Officer Stanton what he'd said, and she saw Mark grimace. "He said I'd ruined Christmas for the kids, that I'd betrayed them, and that I'd never work with kids again."

"You didn't tell me that," Mark said. He didn't sound accusing, just sad.

"It wouldn't have made any difference," she said, glancing up at Mark. "He told me he was taking the kids out for a walk and I'd better be gone by the time he came back. So I packed in a hurry and I left."

"And you didn't touch the necklace again?"

"No. Officer Stanton, the last place I ever want to be again is in that office."

"Thank you, Miss Benedict. I wish you had felt comfortable telling me this from the beginning, but I understand now why you didn't."

"You still would have searched everything."

"It's hard to say. It makes your case much stronger, though, and I think that can only benefit you in the long run. Either I or another Missoula officer will be giving you updates. May we contact you on your phone?"

"Yes." Then she shook her head. "I mean, I'll charge it up."

"And where will you be staying? The reason we're here on Christmas morning is that your sister believed you'd be returning to work tonight or tomorrow. Since they knew there was no job for you to return to, Missoula PD considered you a flight risk."

"I don't know where I'll be."

"When she gets a place I'll know where it is," Mark offered. He shared his phone number and address.

"Think I should find a KOA of my own?" she asked Mark.

"I know a great one," he said with a grin. The officers wrapped up the search fairly quickly, and it only took a glance back at her car to realize that they were doing a better job of packing than she had. Mark shook the snow off the blanket and draped it over his arm. The officers gave each of them a card and left.

She turned off the Subaru, and Mark pulled her into his arms. "You did an awesome job."

"I was a complete idiot."

"You were scared, which makes sense since this whole thing was scary. I have to tell you, I had a hard time keeping quiet. But you did it."

It wasn't just about being scared. Her mind was merely scared—her body was terrified. In turn, that made it hard to think. Was it always going to be like this for her? Would she always be someone that fell exactly when she needed to stand up?

"Nic, look up."

The sky was brightening above them, and she looked up into the clear sky. That was all she saw, the silver blue of the empty sky. But then there was a sparkle. And another. And then the hotel snowplow started up and headlights swept over them.

"Diamond dust."

She knew it was tiny ice crystals, precipitating out of the cloudless sky because of the extreme cold. But it looked like magic.

"It's Christmas," he said, holding her tighter. "Christmas and the cops are gone. What could be better?"

She laughed and watched the tiniest diamonds sparkling in the sky. As far as Christmas presents go, this was a good one.

The cold drove them inside, and they stood by the fire for a while. It was still quiet in the hotel. Her body felt cold and heavy. "I'm tired," she said.

Mark slipped away and came back moments later with two fresh cups of coffee in hand. They headed back to the suite, where he hung the blanket over some stools to dry. Seated in her usual spot on the sofa, Nic looked around. The room looked as if nothing had happened, but it had. And it wasn't over yet, not as angry as Tim Gordon had been.

The suite's phone rang.

Nic ran through the options. Lauren? Tim Gordon? She just wasn't up to talking right now. And as she stared at the phone, wishing it would go away, Mark got up and unplugged it.

"That thing was bugging me," he grumbled. He came back to the sofa and took off his coat, shaping it onto a fluffy pile and setting it on his lap. "Your pillow," he offered. She lay down and closed her eyes, feeling his fingers gently brushing strands of hair from her face. She would lie here just for a moment, she thought.

As she began to stir, the sun shone brightly through her eyelids. She fluttered them a little, just enough to get her bearings. The morning wasn't a dream. She looked up at Mark. He was leaning his head against his hand, watching her.

He looked sad.

"What's wrong?" she asked.

"I was just thinking about how much time I've lost. And this weekend has been a blur." His face transformed. "But I'm glad you're awake. The service is at eleven."

"Service." She sat up and tried to remember the schedule. Something about lunch and a Christmas celebration. She dreaded the thought of being with all the Vangs. "I think I'm going to skip it. It's a family function, after all. But we have one more babysitting job, right? After the service? But they probably won't want to leave kids with me now."

"We'll deal with that. And Nic, I'm the one giving the service."

That surprised her. "I didn't know that."

"Dad asked me to do it in his place. And I want you to come."

"Does that mean he knows about your career change, the seminary, any of it?"

"To be honest, I wouldn't be surprised. They do have their connections. No matter why, I want to do it, and I want you to be there. And I want you to sing 'O Holy Night' with me."

He waited for her answer.

"You're joking, right?" Nic said. "You heard me on the wagon ride. And talking to the police." And you asked that of me last year, then broke up with me.

"Nic, I've sung beside you in church plenty of times. And on hikes, on porches, in cars, hotel rooms, even ice skating on ponds."

"It's not the same."

"Want to know something interesting?" he asked.

She didn't. She wanted him to stop expecting things from her that were unfair to ask. Especially today.

"This came up in one of the seminary chat rooms. So you know God sees everyone, at all times. Past, present, future. And He sees it all at once. So imagine someone singing 'Amazing Grace.' Now think about all the people who have sung it, everywhere in the world, and all the different times they've sung it. Now try to imagine God hearing every single time 'Amazing Grace' has been sung —all at once."

"It's probably a cacophony," she said, but she was trying to imagine it. How many voices? How many versions and languages?

"I think He's got that covered. He created sound, right? I think He can hear it all as one chorus, one symphony. All the little quirks and mistakes and all the heartfelt songs blend together perfectly because it was meant for His ears."

It was a beautiful thought. But she sighed. "What are you trying to say, Mark?"

"Try singing for a different audience. Just Him, the one who made you the way you are. Your performance will be perfect for His choir."

"I might go to the service, Mark. But I can't sing."

"You've done all sorts of amazing things today, Nic. What's one more? Please don't answer now. We've got about an hour. Besides, I need to change into something a little nicer. Knowing Mom, it's a dressy kind of thing."

That made everything seem even worse. She had packed something nice in her bag, but probably not nice enough for the Vang family. As he went to his room, she took a sip of cold coffee and went in to shower.

Even as she dried her hair and put on makeup, she wasn't certain she was going to the service. But she was curious to hear Mark as a "preacher." And Mark had asked her to go. She couldn't refuse him.

Nic put on her opaque black tights and black heels. The heather-gray sweater she'd planned to wear looked nice but was as comfy as a well-worn T-shirt. But she regretted packing that skirt. There should be a rule about not packing clothing items unless you've happily worn them before, she thought. Her friend Ellie had given it to her before she moved to Idaho because, she said, Nic needed to sparkle once in a while. It was a pencil skirt covered entirely in silver sequins.

When Nic had packed it, she'd pictured herself breezing past Mark, looking beautiful and on trend, and then talking to some handsome man. Handsomer than Mark, of course. Once again, her expectations and reality had nothing to do with each other.

And once she had it on, she felt ridiculous. Ellie would have made her do something, though: stare at the mirror, cover the reflection of her face with her hand, and take a more objective look. What kind of girl would wear this outfit? Someone comfortable in her skin. Someone who wasn't afraid to shine.

"Time to go," Mark called. Then more softly, "Please tell me you're going."

She threw the door open, ready to tell him that he'd put entirely too much pressure on her and there was no way she was going, but the expression on his face stopped her.

"Wow."

He said wow.

And she could have said the same thing about him in his gray suit. Of course, he was also wearing Chuck Taylors and a red bowtie, but that was him. Everything had a bright side, even dressing up.

"Wow," he said again. "You look beautiful."

She felt her opportunity to skip the service slipping away.

As if he'd sensed her thoughts, he took her by the hand. "Thank you, Nic. I appreciate it. Promise me you'll laugh at one of my jokes, okay?"

The Vang family had booked the restaurant until one o'clock. Nic walked in feeling good, but right away she noticed a difference in the way people viewed her, and it had nothing to do with sequins. All around her familiar faces glanced her way and then quickly averted their eyes. She hesitated, and Mark squeezed her hand. "Tracie and Melly are waving to us."

"They're at the high table."

He chuckled. "Mom and Dad aren't that bad."

"It's bad enough, and now they think I'm a criminal," she whispered. Mrs. Vang was motioning for them to join her.

"It'll be fun," Mark said. It was his standard statement

about everything. And a fair amount of the time he was right.

She put her shoulders back and walked beside him up to the big table in the bay window. Melly stood up on her chair to give Mark a hug, and then she surprised Nic by giving her one too. Mark pulled out a chair for Nic, and she sat, grateful her back was to the others. She hadn't seen Lauren. Had she and Chris even arrived yet? Nic hoped things weren't so difficult for them that they'd skip the service.

"I was hoping we could get you to sit with us," Mrs. Vang said. Nic was startled to realize she was saying it directly to her. "I was just telling Tracie about your exciting morning. Although I'm sure you'd rather tell her yourself."

No, she thought, crawling into a hole would be preferable.

"He's a pig," Tracie said matter-of-factly. "I'd like to meet him someday in a dark alley. With a Taser."

It took Nic a moment to realize Tracie was talking about Tim Gordon. Mrs. Vang certainly did have her sources. Nic wasn't sure if she felt relieved or offended by how invasive that felt.

"What's a Taser, Mommy?" Melly asked.

"It's like a spanking for really bad men," Tracie said.

Nic turned to Mrs. Vang. "How did you know about it?"

"I had a little talk with Officer Stanton. He said that he couldn't tell me much but that your former employer had lodged a complaint about you. I told him that you had been hired to do childcare and asked if I should be concerned."

Nic tried not to be offended. If the kids were her own, she'd have been tempted to do the same thing.

"He assured me that he believed you were the victim of a crime, not the perpetrator. So I told him that you were my son's fiancée, and he let a few more details slip."

"Mom," Mark said.

Mrs. Vang shrugged, and her burgundy velvet jacket rose and fell neatly back into place. "He was more willing to chat that way."

"I wish you had asked me directly," Nic said. And her voice remained steady as she did.

Mrs. Vang gave her an appraising look. "So do I. Although I did try. No one answered the phone in your room."

Mark raised his hand. "My bad."

"What did you hear?" Nic asked.

Mrs. Vang gave a brief recap. She had the gist of it right, minus the sordid details. "That's pretty much it," she added.

"Pig," Tracie said.

"Oink oink," Melly said. Nic had to smile at that.

Mr. Vang spoke up. "Eliza and I want you to know how much we appreciate you helping out this weekend. Knowing what we know now, it would have been perfectly understandable if you had decided not to come. But you did, and the kids have certainly enjoyed your company."

"She's nice," Melly said.

"Yes, she is," Mark agreed.

"You know," Mrs. Vang said, "Tracie just mentioned that she is looking for a roommate who enjoys children. I was just wondering, have you made arrangements for your next home? Is there any possibility you'd consider moving to Glendive for a short while?"

"Oh," Nic said. She had no idea how to answer that. She wanted so much to look at Mark to see what he thought of his mother inviting his ex-girlfriend to move in down the road, but he sat still and didn't say anything. No one did.

Nic was trying to formulate a lighthearted way to say there was no way on God's green earth she was moving there when Mark spoke up. "I think it's time to start."

Mrs. Vang glanced at her watch and nodded, and Mark slowly stood.

"There are jobs there," Tracie whispered. "Just the basic stuff, you know. Sales, that sort of thing. And teaching. I'd go crazy doing that, but they have a real teacher gap right now. No pressure, of course." She clasped her hands together as if begging and mouthed, "Please?"

Nic smiled, but Mark's silence stung. Her wounded pride wanted to hear him say he would love to have her move to Glendive, but the idea was foolish. For both of them. He was a nice guy who was being kind during a difficult time, and that was the extent of his feelings for her. The more she thought about it, the more certain she was that he'd be relieved to be rid of her.

She glanced at Mrs. Vang. She appeared to be waiting for an answer. It seemed impossible that she'd want to see Nic embroiled in Mark's life again. Everyone agreed that she and Mark weren't good for each other, right?

"Excuse me," Mark said, tapping on a microphone. There were two microphones, one high for him to speak into and one low, for his guitar, she thought. She caught a glimpse of his guitar on a stand behind him. She had no idea he'd brought it. And there was another—did he own two now? She looked again.

It was her guitar.

"Dad asked me to say a few words to help us all center ourselves on this holy day. Although it's kind of ironic to have me tell a room full of moms and dads about the birth of a child."

There was a small ruffle of laughter.

"There is something inherently magical about kids. Mix a little glitter and glue and entire worlds spring into existence. And if you get to play with kids and inhabit those worlds, you find out there's no end to the possibilities. For kids, love is easily given, and so rarely taken away. Unless it's past nap time, of course."

Tracie laughed, along with some of the others. Nic was so preoccupied with her thoughts she didn't even get the joke until the moment had passed.

"Anyone who has had the blessing of loving a child figures out pretty quickly that it's a whole different kind of love," Mark continued. "There's a powerful element of sacrifice to it. And I'm not just talking about the diapers." He made a face. "Or the broken bones—Tegan, I'm talking about you—or any of the tiny hardships that loving parents willingly take on. Eventually, if you do your job right, you send that child off into the world without you. That's real sacrifice. And today marks the sacrifice God made when he gave his only son, and the sacrifice Jesus would be making for each of us."

There was a calm authority about Mark as he read the account of Jesus' birth and spoke about the deeper meanings of the Scripture, the prophecies it fulfilled, and the sacrifice it foretold. Nic stopped thinking about Mark and only thought about what he was saying, and the images in her mind came alive.

Mark loved God. She finally understood what it meant for him to walk away from everyone's expectations for his life—his parents, hers, and his. It wasn't about not caring for them. It was about loving God first.

And the woman he chose to marry would be better off for it.

Nic had heard that advice before, that a woman should seek a man who loves God first and her second, and it had always felt a little like it should apply to other people. She never admitted it out loud, but the idea sounded unromantic. But this—this peaceful, sacrificing, loving version of Mark—made it clear how shortsighted her view was.

Mark had shown faith in her this morning when she least expected him to. Was that why? Because he already had *faith*?

Nic wanted that assurance, more than she wanted him. She wanted to be able to trust when things got awful and humiliating. She even wanted to believe that when her voice wavered, God heard something beautiful.

"Nic." Mark's voice over the microphone jolted her out of her reverie. "Would you mind playing 'O Holy Night' with me?"

What if I panic? Nic thought.

What if I don't?

She stood up and walked over to him. It was as if thoughts were buzzing in the back of her head, but there was a distance between them and where she was. As she came over, Mark pulled up two empty chairs and arranged them so that they faced each other. Tricky, she thought. She didn't care what the others thought of the arrangement. She sat down with her back to the audience, facing Mark.

Okay, God. I don't care what the Vangs think. I don't even care what Mark thinks. But I don't want to miss this last chance to play with him because I think what we create is beautiful. I hope you think so too.

He handed her guitar to her and took up his own. She was conscious of the microphone to her left, but she didn't let her mind linger there. Mark set up the sheet music, though she knew it by heart.

He waited for her. And when she felt ready, she strummed the beautiful hymn she loved so much.

O holy night! The stars are brightly shining,
It is the night of our dear Savior's birth.
Long lay the world in sin and error pining,
'Til He appear'd and the soul felt its worth.

How that last line moved her. What a beautiful thought, that we were valuable long before we felt valuable.

A thrill of hope, the weary world rejoices,
For yonder breaks a new and glorious morn.

She hadn't decided to sing along, to blend her voice in harmony with his, but how could she not sing?

. . .

Fall on your knees! O hear the angel voices!
O night divine, O night when Christ was born;
O night divine, O night, O night Divine.

The next verse she sang alone. She could feel the anxiety within, like an alarm going off in the distance, but she concentrated on the song, matching Mark, watching his fingers on the guitar. It was like a river they could tap into, a rhythm all its own, one they both knew and followed. She could feel herself lead here, and Mark leading there, each doing their part to follow the current.

Led by the light of Faith serenely beaming,
With glowing hearts by His cradle we stand.
So led by light of a star sweetly gleaming,
Here come the wise men from the Orient land.
The King of Kings lay thus in lowly manger;
In all our trials born to be our friend.

And the strength in her voice when he joined her in harmony. It felt so good to stretch out her voice, to test it and find no trace of quavering. I was made for this, she thought.

He knows our need, to our weaknesses no stranger,
Behold your King! Before Him lowly bend!
Behold your King, Before Him lowly bend!

. . .

Mark would take the next verse, just as they'd planned to do a year ago. Neither of them had to say a word. He remembered.

Truly He taught us to love one another;
His law is love and His gospel is peace.
Chains shall He break for the slave is our brother;
And in His name all oppression shall cease.
Sweet hymns of joy in grateful chorus raise we,
Let all within us praise His holy name.

Christ is the Lord! O praise His Name forever,
His power and glory evermore proclaim.
His power and glory evermore proclaim.

Nic's fingers were effortless on the frets. It was as if she could hear echoes of the notes before she played them, she was so certain. If she made mistakes, it didn't matter. They drifted away before she could regret them.

Everything grew quieter as they sang the refrain one last time, and then the song was finished.

No one made a sound. And when she realized that, she felt panic seeping into her veins. Mark tapped her on her knee. "Turn around."

She was about to shake her head. But instead she shot a quick look over her left shoulder, and there, where she hadn't seen her before, was Lauren. She was smiling. And wiping tears from her eyes.

Nic felt honored. Some songs were so beautifully

inspiring. As wonderful as it was to hear them, it was even more amazing to be part of making that music.

"I hope you'll all join us in the next two songs," Mark said into the microphone. "There are a couple of copies of the words on each table." As he spoke, he reached over and changed the music on her stand. They played and sang "Emmanuel" and "Joy to the World."

Tegan was her favorite singer. He sang long and loud, regardless of whether he was in the correct key. If Mark was right about God's choir, Tegan just might be a soloist. When it was over, everyone applauded enthusiastically and Mark gestured to the table.

But Nic didn't make it to the table. The same woman who had served them her first lunch put a hand on her arm as she passed. "Miss Benedict? There is a call for you at the front desk. They said it was urgent."

Back into the fire, she thought. "I'll be fine," she assured Mark, and she went out into the lobby. The host there called her to walk behind the front desk and into a slightly more private spot against the back wall.

"Thank you for taking my call," the woman said. It was strained and low, but Nic immediately recognized Marie Gordon's voice.

"Of course," Nic said.

"The police called, but I didn't believe them. Tim got so angry he went out for a walk. I was just trying to put the plastic wrap in the trash."

Nic had no idea what she was talking about, but she could hear the strain in the woman's voice, so she listened.

"My watch bumped against the lid and it fell off, right into the garbage. You know how much I hate the trash.

But it isn't waterproof. And it was a gift." Marie Gordon's voice broke for a moment, and then she continued. "Tim gave me that watch last Christmas. So I put on a pair of rubber gloves and reached inside, and I felt it. But when I pulled it out, I realized I'd grabbed a necklace. Wrapped in a paper towel."

Nic closed her eyes.

"I just took out the trash yesterday morning. I wanted to think it was an accident, but how else do you explain it being there in today's trash? A twelve-thousand-dollar necklace tossed in the garbage. After he had said it was stolen. That's how much he loves his reputation, Nic. He loves it so much more than me. I've known it all along."

"I'm sorry, Marie," Nic said.

"I don't know what to do."

Nic could hear the familiar shallow breathing that accompanied withheld tears.

"I told him to leave. And now it's Christmas, Daddy's gone, and you're gone, and they want you so much, Nic. I can't stand how much this is hurting them."

Nic blinked back tears. She too hated the thought of it.

"I'm sorry," Marie went on. "It all sounded wrong from the very beginning, but I didn't stand up for you. He's my husband. I just couldn't imagine. I know it would be so much to ask, but if you could return to Missoula today..."

Christmas with Petra and Elliot? Or even her old job back? She was only a couple hours away. She could be there in time to make cookies—for children that were not hers. In a household desperately in need of healing, she would be a reminder of their darkest time.

"Marie, they don't miss me," Nic said. "They miss you."

Muffled sounds muted the phone for a moment, and

when Marie spoke again, Nic could tell she'd been crying hard. "I miss them too. Sometimes I feel like I don't know them. Or Tim."

"I don't know that it helps, but nothing happened between your husband and me. Maybe he's just gone off the rails. Maybe ..." Nic didn't know, and she didn't have the right to know, but three last words just slipped out. "He needs Jesus."

Great. Now she sounded like the late-night TV preachers who scream at crowds of adoring fans, "Sinner, you need Jesus!" But a fact was a fact. It was so simple and clear that it bordered on cliché. But that was the difference between a man like Mark and a man like Tim. Both were human, both sinners. She never saw Tim's faith, but Mark's faith was in everything he did.

God, if you want me married someday, please help me to find a man who loves You.

"I believe you," Marie said. "Isn't that horrible? I believe you, but I can't believe a word he says." She sighed. "You aren't coming back, are you?"

"No." Yesterday the answer would have been different. But things had changed. It was strange to realize how much she didn't want to go back. "But I miss them too. Will you tell them for me? I left presents for them. Just tell them they're in a hiding place." Nic stopped. She wasn't going to tell Marie what to do now; she couldn't even imagine her pain. She was just going to pray for wisdom for her and peace for her kids.

"I told the police, Nic. They're considering prosecuting. And the insurance company is going to be furious. I just wanted you to know that I know. I don't want to pile this on the kids, so I just told them you needed to be with your family. That you miss them."

I do, so much, Nic thought. But they needed their mom. Especially now. "Thank you, Marie."

"Thanks again for taking the call. I thought you'd be... never mind. If I have any questions, can I text you? Please?"

"Of course."

After a couple awkward pauses and short good-byes, the call was over. Nic hadn't seen that coming.

Neither did she expect to turn around and find Lauren standing in front of her, wringing a cloth napkin in her hands and looking awful. "Is everything okay?" she asked.

"It's good," Nic answered.

"I was worried."

"I know," Nic said. "I wish you wouldn't."

"Well, that's not going to happen," Lauren said.

"You're probably right." Nic stepped forward to give her sister a hug, and Lauren clung to her.

"I'm sorry, Nic. We both said awful things."

"It's okay," Nic said. It didn't hurt anymore, not when she realized there was so much more going on in Lauren and Chris's life than she suspected. "I need to apologize. I'm always telling you not to boss me around, but I haven't ever said how glad I am that you stepped up when Mom died."

Lauren clung even tighter.

"I can do it, Lauren." Life, the job, the police, whatever. She would find a way. "I want you to have more faith in me."

Lauren backed away, and Nic could see a great debate

taking shape in Lauren's mind. But all Lauren said was, "I'll try."

"Will you stop bossing me around?"

"Probably not," she answered.

Nic smiled, and they hugged again. It felt good. It felt like they were sisters. Here was another amazing Christmas present, Nic thought.

"They already served the meal," Lauren said. Nic walked back in with her and caught Chris's sheepish look. Then she went back to her spot at the high table. It was filled with plates of food, but no one had eaten.

"Mark, will you please do the honor?" Mrs. Vang said. Nic took Mark's and Melly's hands. They'd waited to say grace until she had arrived.

Mark said something short and sweet, just like his father, and then everyone took silverware in hand. Nic hoped for their sakes it was still hot, and it was.

"We've been placing bets on who called," Mr. Vang said, deadpan as ever.

"Bob, shame on you," Mrs. Vang said. "Don't worry, no money exchanged hands."

Mark made a wry face, but his eyes never left Nic. He looked concerned.

"It was Marie Gordon. The necklace turned up. Tim left the house, and she asked me to come back."

To her side, she saw Mark lower his head a little. If he had an opinion about that request, he kept it to himself.

"What did you say?" Tracie asked.

"I said no."

It seemed as if Mark's head and shoulders bowed down a little lower. Was he disappointed?

"I think that's wise," Mrs. Vang said. "There's no telling if she'll decide tomorrow to let him back home."

"It is his home," Mr. Vang said. "He has a legal claim."

She stopped herself from asking Mark if he thought she'd made a mistake. It was her decision to make, regardless of what he thought. And she was sure it was the right one, no matter what came of it.

Tracie, who had been talking Melly into trying the cranberry sauce, leaned over and whispered, "I'm glad, Nic. And not just because I want you to move in with me."

"You don't even know what horrible household habits I might have."

"Whatever. Melly likes you, and I trust her judgment." She scowled. "Then again, you might be sick of the idea of hanging out with other people's kids, after the way things have gone for you this week."

"I think I'm over the nanny job," Nic said. "I don't want to raise other people's kids *for* them. I don't think it's good for anyone. Even with the awesome pay. I can't remember the last time I got to take a weekend trip."

"Well, you wouldn't have to worry about that. I'd be just fine anytime you and Mark want to go camping."

The table was silent. Tracie looked up at Mark with feigned surprise. "What? You guys are adorable together. Even reindeer think you're irresistible." She flashed a brilliant smile.

Nic wanted to see Mark's reaction, but she was afraid of what she'd find. She shook her head and smiled as if it was all just a silly joke, but there was a weight on her heart. Everything was... okay. There was just enough peace with Lauren, with the Gordons, with the police, and even with her future. And yet she felt weighed down.

She took a few bites of food and was grateful when Mrs. Vang changed the topic. She was so conscious of Mark beside her. He was the one place she wouldn't look, the one person she couldn't talk to, and yet she felt as if she would do anything to have him say something to her. Just a few friendly words, or a gentle touch, just to let her know they were still friends.

But that wouldn't ease her feelings. Nic was aware that Mr. Vang had said a joke, and she smiled, but it was as if the conversation around her was muted. She felt caught in Mark's gravity, revolving around him but never coming closer. She'd toyed with her own heart, and now she was in love with him. Again. Or maybe it had never gone away.

There was no way on earth she would move in with Tracie and her adorable daughter. Move to the eastern plains and live in a tiny town where she could see Mark every single day? She wasn't foolish enough to do that. Not that she'd ever entertained the idea, anyway. Nic had made up her mind. And that made her feel strong and independent. But in the back of her mind was a tiny voice saying, *This is wrong.*

Wrong or not, it was reality. She could move to Great Falls. Or Billings, Montana's largest city. There would be so many possibilities there. She would find a way to work with kids that preserved her independence and her free time. It could be anything. Guitar instructor, daycare worker, lifeguard. The possibilities were endless.

"Mommy said, are you okay?"

It was the touch of Melly's hand on her arm that broke her out of her reverie. Nic smiled at Tracie. "Yeah, it's just been a big day."

"No joke," Tracie said. "And now you get to take the whole herd sledding. Are you sure you're going to be okay?"

"You don't have to go," Mark said. "I can cover for you if you want to rest."

Finally he'd spoken, and it was to tell her that he didn't need her around. Nic hid her true reaction and said, "That's kind of you."

Mark nodded and looked down at his plate again. That was where his attention had been for most of the meal, but he hadn't even eaten half his Christmas supper.

When the dessert order came around, Nic asked for pumpkin pie. Just because. Without cheese. It arrived smothered in whipped cream, and she took a bite. It was smooth and spicy and delicious, and she could hardly eat a quarter of it. It was as if her stomach had been irretrievably trained to digest apple pie, and anything else wasn't welcome. Nic decided that she wouldn't eat apple pie again for a while. Maybe a year. It was time to break old habits and find new favorites. She was too young to be so stuck in her ways.

Mark sat upright. "Sorry to say this, but we should go." For someone who had been so quiet, he sounded awfully energetic all of a sudden.

Nic followed his lead, thanking the Vangs for the meal. Nic got a good-bye hug from Melly, who cheerfully said, "See you later, alligator." Nic wasn't certain if that was true, but she didn't say otherwise. By early tomorrow, most everyone would be gone.

She had almost made it across the restaurant when Mark grabbed her hand. He was just a touchy-feely kind of guy, she thought. She knew better than to mistake his affection for something more.

He tugged her over to the table where Chris and Lauren were sitting alone. Chris cleared his throat and addressed them both. "I need to apologize for what I said. It was unfounded and rude."

Nic wondered if those were his words or Lauren's. Either way, they sounded heartfelt.

"That's not good enough," Mark said. "I think there's something you need to do for us."

Nic realized she was still holding Mark's hand. When she tried to draw her hand away, his grip tightened a little.

Chris eyed him cautiously. "Yes?"

"I think you and Lauren should take all the kids sledding this afternoon."

"You do," the older brother said.

"Yes, I do. As an apology, and because I think it would be excellent practice for both of you."

Lauren stared at Mark with wide eyes. Chris's lips thinned to a narrow line.

"Done," Lauren said.

Chris winced.

"Excellent," Mark said with a smile. "Have a great time."

"And Mark," Lauren said, "Your service today was wonderful. It meant a lot to me."

Mark thanked her. He dropped Nic's hand and rubbed the back of his neck as they walked toward the stairs. Nic had been so wrapped up in her phone call and her blue mood that she hadn't said a word to Mark about the service. She felt ashamed. And she felt as if anything she said now would seem insincere. She wanted to tell him how sweet his words had been to hear, and how humbling. Instead, she walked in silence. Mark opened the door of the suite for her and started pacing the floor. "Um," he started twice, and then he finally stopped and faced her. "I need to talk to you."

Was there ever a pleasurable conversation that started that way? Fine, he could tell her all the reasons they should go back to their separate lives without a second thought, but first she'd get this burden off of herself.

"Mark, before you do, I want you to know how much I appreciated the service today. And not just singing with you. Although that was beautiful. I appreciated what you said. And the way you said it."

He gave her a wry smile. "You like the cheesy jokes."

"Maybe. Yes. But I'm not talking about that. I'm talking about your insight. How you linked so many things together. It didn't just make today seem like Christmas; it made me think of all the Christmases that have come before, and how different the world is." She had talked herself into a corner. She didn't have the words to tell him all the thoughts and images his sermon had sparked in her mind. So she just said, "This is what you're meant to do."

He exhaled. She could see the tension leaking out of his body. "Thank you."

They stood there, just looking at each other while she waited to hear whatever he intended to say.

"You don't know what it was like for me, sitting in there, thinking you'd be driving back to Missoula at any moment, and the way you kept dodging Tracie's invitation." He ran his fingers through his hair. "Just give me a moment. I need to find something," he said.

Frustrated and dreading their "talk," she went into her

room to fish the necklace out of her coat pocket. She really should have found a way to wrap it. All she could do now was wrap a couple layers of facial tissue around it and use red thread from the Boredom Bag to tie a bow. It looked silly. But she held it behind her back and came out into the living room just the same.

Mark was standing there with his arms crossed. In the middle of the coffee table was the tiny box she had seen in his suitcase. He looked more anxious than she had ever seen him look before. She sat down on the couch and tried not to stare at the box. The ribbons were terribly askew. She was sure the police had searched inside. After all, it did look like a jewelry box.

He took off his jacket. "I got you a present. It looks pretty bad, I know."

"Not any worse than this," she said, and she placed his present on the coffee table.

He grinned. For a moment, he looked like himself, but it didn't last. "I have to explain. I've been carrying this present around for a long time. I mean, everywhere, Nic. I've had it with me every single day for, well, more than a year."

He came around the coffee table and sat down facing her so that the box was hidden behind his back. "I was going to give this to you last Christmas Eve. I had it all planned out. And I wanted… I can't tell you how much I wanted…" His words trailed away, and he looked down at his hands.

"I even brought it to Chris's wedding," he managed. "But you looked so happy. You looked relieved. And I knew it just wasn't right to drag you through my stupid little life crisis. I got out of your way, Nic, but my mind never changed. Every single day since then I've had this with me. And every day I've wanted to give it to you." Finally, he handed her the box.

She slid the ribbons off and lifted the lid. Inside was a simple gold ring, with one modest, sparkling diamond in a rosette setting. It was romantic and elegant, and just the opposite of the tall and heavy rings her friends coveted. She'd never seen anything so beautiful.

It was a ring. She looked up at him. "A ring?"

He nodded. "It's an engagement ring. I wanted to ask you to marry me last year, Nic, but I realized I wasn't going to be the kind of man I was raised to be. The Vang entrepreneur. The steady provider." He shook his head. "I knew my heart was in ministry, but the wife of a minister is a ministry in itself. I had to be sure I was on the right path before I ever thought of asking you to walk it with me."

She was dumbfounded. "An engagement ring."

"I was hoping, Nic, but I'm not stupid enough to expect you'll accept it as that now. I know how much I hurt you because I felt the same way. But it's yours. No matter what, it belongs to you."

She couldn't speak. She just sat there, staring at it, afraid even to take it out of the box.

After a while, Mark leaned over and took his present in his hands and tore away the tissue. She heard his breath catch, and she looked up to see the amazed expression on his face. "I can't believe you remembered," he said softly.

"Of course I did. I love you." The words just fell out. But she didn't regret them. Mark didn't say a thing. When she looked at him again, she saw the hope in his eyes, and finally everything started to fall into place.

"You love me," he said. There was the rogue's grin. "You love me. Does that mean... Nic, we could have a long engagement. We'd go through all the premarital counseling and figure out all the details and make sure you could stand to be with me, I promise, but if you would be willing to move to Glendive, you know you have a place waiting for you at Tracie's, and..."

She shrugged. "You haven't even asked me."

With one strong shove, he swept the coffee table back and dropped to one knee. "Nicole Benedict, I have loved you since the first moment I saw you. You are the first thing I think about in the morning, and I want yours to be the last face I see every night for the rest of my life. Everything I do I want to do with you. Please marry me."

All her anxiety was gone. And she understood at last how the most exciting things could make a person feel still. Peaceful. "Yes."

He stood and pulled her to her feet and wrapped her in a crushing hug. He said her name, then kissed her.

This kiss wasn't like any Nic could remembered. She'd kissed Mark before, but not like this. There was a new strength in his hands, and one tangled in her hair while one arm wrapped around her to pull her close. She remembered his gentleness, but not the breathless urgency underneath his kiss. When he finally stopped, she felt dizzy.

Then she laughed. "Oh boy. What is your family going to say?"

"You might be surprised. We'll do this right, Nic. The one thing you know for sure about me is that I'll wait for you, as long as you need. But if I have my way, I'll never spend another day apart from you again."

"You're already keeping me waiting for another kiss," she teased. Mark gave her the rogue's grin and pulled her into his arms.

I've missed you, her heart sang.

~~ The End ~~

AFTERWORD

Alhambra, Montana, is now officially a subdivision that shares a zip code with Clancy, Montana. But during the gold rush, Alhambra was a resort town in its own right, sporting two large hotels that lured tourists off the train and into the warm water of the local hot spring. For this story I imagined the Alhambra Hotel as still standing, inviting guests onto its wrapped porch, and that its tiny pond had been developed. I pictured the hotel restored and even enlarged. I even imagined that the surrounding forest, which was denuded as the mining industry moved in, still remained.

But the truth is that the Alhambra Hotel burned down in 1959 and a new structure stands in its place, although the town still exists. I once lived in a town that had lost its status and been deemed a mere "subdivision," and I can tell you this—a town is more than a post office and a separate zip code. It's a shared history and a state of mind.

As for Montana hot springs, you should know that the state boasts all sorts of hot springs and vapor caves, many of which are close to Alhambra. Some have their grand old buildings intact, some are newer constructions, and others are just pools along the river at the end of a remote trail. There's something for everyone, with and without the unusually high levels of radon of Alhambra's hot spring!

Many thanks to the www.HelenaHistory.org website, "Helena As She Was." It was on that site that I found the old photos of Alhambra that got my wheels turning in the first place.

MORE FROM CYNTHIA BRUNER

For a free short story, please visit www.cynthiabruner.com and sign up for my newsletter. I won't spam you or sell your address, but we will give you first crack at special deals and upcoming books. And I love hearing from my readers!

I could also use your help. Customer reviews help other readers find books that are a match for them, and they're the sparkle on an author's Christmas tree, the ice under her skates, and the jingle in her bells. Please leave a review where you purchased this book!

Made in the USA
Columbia, SC
25 April 2019